GABRIELLE MARIE KOZAK

Killing Time

First edition

ISBN: 978-1-970936-16-2

This book was professionally typeset on Reedsy.
Find out more at reedsy.com

"It hurts, doesn't it. That's why I chose to forget.
You might as well start forgetting now."

— VIRA

Contents

1

What happened? I don't know… I'm still half asleep, I guess… My arm hurts, my neck and back, too…

Where am I? This is totally not my bedroom ceiling. Tile, with lights that hurt my eyes…

"Where am I?" I manage to whisper. My lips are covered in something dried…blood? It hurts to move my face.

I blink as someone comes into view. A nurse?

Am I in the hospital?

"You're awake!" she smiles brightly. "How are you feeling, Ms. Thyme? Do you remember what happened?"

Suddenly I sit bolt upright as the memories come back to me. "Where are my parents?" I ask urgently, panic in my voice. "Where are they?"

"Hey, you're going to be okay, Ms. Thyme. Lie back down, please. You'll get to see your parents later."

But the smile has already faded from her face.

"No," I scream. "No!"

I shut my eyes tightly, reliving the crash. Mom and Dad are in the front of the car… I'm in the back, laughing about how Dad knew exactly what coffee I wanted. It tastes so good… My Dad is awesome.

Then we turn the corner. Impact.

Mom and Dad smash forward but their seat belts stop them. I slam my head on the back of Dad's seat and black out, my own scream fading away in my ears.

The nurse is tapping my shoulder. I open my eyes again and let the tears flow.

"I'm sorry, Elvira." Her voice is so frigidly gentle.

I hate it. Or do I just hate the words?

"Your parents didn't make it."

* * *

I don't know what to do.

I'm lying awake, even though it's past 2 AM. I'm not crying anymore. My eyes feel dead. My mind feels even more dead.

Please tell me this is just a dream… My parents are dead. I have no other relatives. I'm only eighteen. I haven't even started my first job.

I am all alone.

My parents… I squeeze my eyes shut, grabbing my chest. My heart hurts…

O God, help me… What am I going to do?

The nurse comes in again. I hear her move around in the room, but I don't react. Somehow she can see I'm awake anyway.

"Can you try to eat something?" she asks me. Her voice is new. She must be someone else. "Please?"

"I want to die," I whisper, my voice cracking.

"What was that?" She leans close to the bed.

I open my eyes. "No."

Don't want her to think I'm suicidal or something.

Am I, though?

"Look; I brought you a protein bar. And a yogurt parfait. And…chocolate." Her smile isn't very convincing.

"I don't want to eat," I scowl.

"Well, you're an adult. I can't make you take care of yourself. But I *can* put you on an IV if you won't take in nutrition the normal way."

I sigh. I have absolutely no appetite, but she has a point.

"Fine."

Next thing I know there's a tray on my blanket-covered lap. To my surprise, the nurse sits down on the bed next to me. "Is there any music you like, honey? A movie, maybe?"

At 2 AM? This is one interesting hospital nurse.

"I like Aurora," I manage after a minute. "I... I don't want to watch any shows."

Not without Mom and Dad, anyway.

"Alright. Do you want to talk instead?" She gets a remote and starts up the wall TV. In the new, faint light I can see her more clearly. She's tall, with short blonde hair. Her earrings are little gold hoops and she's not wearing any makeup.

She's really pretty. My chest aches as I remember Mom and how she dresses when she goes out with Dad...

How she *dressed* when she went out with Dad.

"Maybe," I concede, blinking the thought away.

I'm starting to like this new nurse. Despite everything...she comforts me, somehow. "Don't you have somewhere you have to be?"

"I'm all here for you, sweetheart," she smiles, clicking *Play*. "For as long as you need me. Wow, I never thought I'd see a teenager take so long to eat a bar of chocolate."

I have to repress a giggle. Yeah, this nurse is great.

Slowly I unwrap the bar and take a bite.

"So you're eighteen," the nurse muses. "I'm sorry for you, dear."

"What's your name?" I ask. She's not wearing a badge like the other nurse was.

In fact...she's not even wearing a uniform. I stop chewing and stare.

She laughs. "I'm off duty right now, but I heard about you and wanted to come see if I could help. My name is Lucie Bernard. You can call me Lucie."

"Lucie," I repeat after her thoughtfully.

The chocolate is really good, after all. And so is this Lucie. What kind of hospital nurse comes in at 2 AM, when she doesn't have to be working, to see a teenager?

I'm beginning to like her. She's like…

Mom.

The word bites into my stomach, and I wince. But Lucie is watching me.

"You're going to be okay," she tells me, her voice gentle and soft.

Like Mom's when she used to tell me bedtime stories. Bedtime stories about the little redhaired girl she loved.

"You're going to live through this, Elvira Thyme. You're a fighter."

* * *

"I still don't completely get what's going on, but from what you're telling me, this is our best opportunity to round him up." The police chief shrugged. "Seems heartless, but so is murdering a hundred people in cold blood, as our friend the Slayer has done. What's that?"

"Sir, it's not…" The reporting officer seemed reluctant to say something.

"What?" John Bellner wasn't one to beat around the bush, and he hated it when people tried to do it.

"It's a her, sir."

John sat down in his chair. Rather suddenly. "What?" His face twisted in confusion. "A her?"

"Yes. An eighteen-year-old by name of Elvira Thyme."

"That's impossible." John's mind was quick; that was why he was Chief of Police in the Southern States. "That's quite literally…impossible."

Here was one crazy case.

Slayer. That was what he'd been known as for the past ten years.

The man who killed his victims with some kind of weapon the world had not yet seen. A totally silent gun that killed at ridiculous distances. Shot with incredible aim from random office buildings located in high-rise cities around the United States.

The targets were always totally random. The only clue the police had discovered was in a room they'd traced the trajectory angle to find. There was one empty bullet shell on the floor. And on it…a single fingerprint and the word *Slayer*.

The fingerprint had never been seen before. Not until a month ago, when some totally random person had gotten their fingerprints taken, probably never dreaming that they'd left one on a crime scene ten years before. Only recently had this case ended up at John's doorstep, so he couldn't be blamed for not yet knowing all the details about this particular one. After all, he had to handle all the biggest cases of crime in the Southern Territory.

So this killer…renowned among the police forces of the country…was an eighteen-year-old girl.

As if he could read John's thoughts, the policeman nodded. "Yeah. And her life story makes it even more confusing."

"Get me the files," John ordered simply, leaning back in his chair and shutting his eyes.

The man ducked out of the room.

John had been on the police force for the past thirty years, and he'd never in his life come across a conundrum like this one.

The Slayer. Serial killer. The second most wanted man in the United States.

He was a *teenage girl*.

No. That didn't make any sense. Fifteen years ago was the first recorded crime of the Slayer. The suspect would've been three years old.

Absolutely ridiculous.

But no two person's fingerprints were the same. That just didn't happen. Ever.

"Good heavens," John mumbled. What was he supposed to do? What was going on?

The suspect had been watched closely for the past month as the police waited for the opportune moment to arrest the assassin. Now was the time, it seemed. The suspect was hospitalized and enduring the shock of losing both parents.

An eighteen-year-old girl.

Fingerprints were evidence. And this was their only suspect for the Slayer.

They had to do it. Impossible as it seemed…they had to make sure.

John picked up his phone and dialed a number.

"Time to arrest the Slayer."

* * *

What?

Oh. I was just asleep.

Asleep?

The clock reads *5:48.* No one is around. Lucie had to go over an hour ago. I guess I fell asleep reading the book she left me.

What woke me up?

None of the machines in the room are making noise…

There's that sound again.

I look over towards the door. I think someone's knocking on it… They must want to be let in.

Still half-asleep, I slip out of bed and over to the door. My hospital slippers are strangely loud on the floor… I glance down at myself and freeze. I'm in an extremely wrinkled purple hospital gown. Am I really in any shape to let anyone in?

Wait…who wants to get in, anyway?

Suddenly I find that my brain is working again. It's 5:50, and I'm in hospital room alone.

Nurses wouldn't knock. Lucie didn't have to knock.

My heart rate suddenly speeds up to twice the pace it was at before. I back away from the door and look at all the machines in panic. Somewhere there's got to be something to call for help…

I find the device plugged into the bed and hit the emergency button. "Help! Someone's trying to get into the room!" I hiss into it as quietly as I can manage.

I listen in shock as the person at the other end tries to cover a cold laugh. "Really?"

"Who are you?" I demand. What is going on?

No one answers, and just then the door flies open. I drop the phone-like device and turn to face the doorway.

A tall figure stands there, completely clothed in black. What…who…

The person lifts something, and the faint light from the computer desk glances off it. A gun…?

Am I about to die?

"No," I whisper, my knees suddenly shaking. I'm alone…defenseless… What is going on? Oh God, help me… Have You decided You want me to follow my parents this way?

But the person seems surprised. "You…you don't *want* to die?"

It's a woman… What? Who is she and why is she trying to kill me?

I don't *want* to die?

My parents are gone… But there's still hope, I decide, and cling to it frantically.

No, I don't want to die. Even if Lucie is the only one who cares for me. Even if she doesn't.

Because God loves me!

And yet I am afraid to die! Am I really ready?

The woman's gun clicks softly, and I shut my eyes tightly. This is it, then… I'm a broken, battered teen. My life has just started and stopped with an abrupt crash—literally. I'm going to die…alone…

There is no sound, but the woman's arm with the gun jerks. I look down to see blood spreading all over the hospital gown.

It hurts…so bad… I fall down, gasping.

"Oh." The woman's voice sounds strange in my ears. "That…doesn't work."

There's that sound again.

I look over towards the door. I think someone's knocking on it…

Wait…*who* wants to get in?

Hang on. It's 5:50, and I'm in hospital room—alone.

My heart rate suddenly speeds up to twice the pace it was at before. I back away from the door and look at all the machines in panic. Isn't there supposed to be something to call for help?

I find the device plugged into the bed and hit the emergency button. "Someone…someone's here," I hiss into it as quietly as I can manage.

I listen in shock as the person at the other end tries to cover a cold laugh. "Really?"

I freeze, the device in my hand. What is going on?

The door flies open. I drop the device and turn to face the doorway.

There's a tall figure completely dressed in black. What...who...

The person lifts something, and the faint light from the computer desk glances off it. A gun...?

"No," I whisper, my knees shaking. I'm alone...defenseless...

The figure walks over to me slowly...

Suddenly I regain possession of myself, and look around wildly for some path of escape. There is only the window...but that's got to be better than being shot in cold blood.

I hope the glass isn't super strong or something, I tell myself as I make a sudden dash for it, throwing Lucie's book ahead of me, as hard as I can. It doesn't break. I run full speed into the full-height window. Well, as fast as I can in the five feet of room. Flailing my fists and screaming, I try to break through it.

My attacker grabs me from behind and throws me to the floor. I scream one more time.

"How—"

It's a woman's voice. But whatever she's trying to say gets abruptly interrupted.

"Hands in the air or we open fire!"

The police?

The woman hits something on her wrist and...vanishes.

I spin around to face the doorway.

Someone's standing there. Someone in black...and holding a...gun?

Am I about to die?

"No," I whisper, my knees suddenly shaking.

Oh God, help me... What is this?

The person's gun clicks softly, and his arm jerks away as a noiselessly shot bullet tinkles into the window behind where my head just was. Two more follow, but I have partially regained control of myself, and I scramble under the bed. Why, I don't know. It's just a matter of time before...

"I don't understand!"

It's a *woman?*

Suddenly she runs towards the window, smashing through it and out into whatever's past it.

I hold my breath. Did she seriously just *leave?*

I feel myself all over, but nothing's hurt except my shoulder. It's grazed or something and the blood is coming fast, but it's not going to kill me. I slowly crawl out from underneath the bed, then stand up to see what'll happen if I try to go out into the hallway and find help.

"Hands in the air!"

There are policemen in the doorway. I breathe a sigh of relief. "Tha—"

"Last chance—hands in the air!"

Suddenly it dawns on me that the officer in front is addressing…*me?*

Slowly I reach for the sky.

I am so confused… What?

They surround me. I can't figure out what's going on.

Someone just tried to kill me. And now *I'm* being arrested? I don't get it… "Miss Thyme." One of the men steps forward as the rest take their hands off their weapons. I stare at him. He's not that old…rather young, actually. Looks rather Italian, but that's just a detail my confused brain pulls out of the much more relevant picture:

I'm under arrest.

I'm…

Under arrest.

2

"Hey, yes, I'm on my way to work. Did you need something?" The twenty-five-year-old Italian-American FBI agent put his phone on speakerphone and laid it down next to him so he could concentrate on driving. Normally he didn't take calls while driving, but something from his girlfriend was not to be ignored.

"So what's with the attempted murder?"

Pietro Dola's eyebrows shot up. "What do you know about that?" he demanded, a little bit of a Southern Italian accent coming into his voice. "That was supposed to be—"

The woman on the other end laughed lightly, though tensely. "Elvira Thyme is a friend of mine, Pietro. And I want to know that she's being properly taken care of. That's all. So what's the deal?"

"Lucie, I can't tell you anything, and you know that." Pietro took one hand off the steering wheel to run it through his thick, black hair. "It's illegal."

"Just tell me you're going to help her." Lucie Bernard smiled on her end of the phone. She knew Pietro wouldn't let her down.

"Alright." Pietro sighed. "I will help her...if I can."

"How early did you get up today?" Lucie changed the topic suddenly. Pietro had not sounded so tired in a long time.

"Pretty early. Okay, I'll call you back at lunch break, okay?" Pietro

bit his lip.

"Okay. Bye."

"Bye." Pietro listened until he heard the hang-up tone.

"*Dai!*" he muttered in Italian annoyance as he pulled into the sheriffs' office parking lot.

* * *

I'm saying the Rosary...over and over again. It never had much meaning for me. It doesn't now. I say the words but there is no meaning behind them. But I'm sure that Our Lady is listening anyway. Because she's the only one there to listen. She and God...are the only ones I have left.

I'm trying to process...but nothing makes sense.

My parents are dead. I've been shot at. And then arrested.

All within 24 hours.

I've been lying awake on some little sick-bay style bed for some time now... They asked me a few questions once we got here and they changed the bandage on my shoulder—around 6:30. Mostly about the attack right before I got picked up. I'd never seen police looking so confused in my life. Well, I guess I hadn't seen many police before.

Now the clock reads 8:00. This time yesterday I was at the beach with my parents...

I've got no tears left to cry, or I would. Everything has happened so suddenly that none of it seems real. I don't understand...

Someone taps on the door. I sit bolt upright on the cot. A moment later the door is slowly pushed open, and a young secretary looks in.

"Miss Thyme?" she asks softly. "Agent Dola would like to speak with you."

I look down at my hospital gown, and suddenly the secretary smiles. "Give me a minute. I'll get you some proper clothes, young lady."

After I change, I stuff the hospital gown under the pillow of the cot. I already feel a little fresher... The bandage on my shoulder isn't too big and it isn't hurting that much anymore, though that's probably due to the drugs they gave me.

I thump the door to tell the secretary that I'm ready, and it opens a few seconds later. The cop—agent?—who talked to me at the hospital steps into the room, a folder in his hand. The secretary follows him, and I'm glad for that. I don't want to be in a room alone with a man I don't know…this situation is already bad enough.

"Good morning, Miss Thyme. Have you been able to rest at all?" Agent Dola's face is surprisingly kind, though tired.

I nod briefly to answer his question, though I don't think I actually slept at all.

He sits down in one of the empty chairs, and the secretary takes the other one. I sit down on the cot after a minute. Looks like this is going to be a serious conversation.

"Can I start by confirming some basic details about you?" the agent asks, opening his folder and pulling a pen out of his pocket. "After we're finished, I'll ask you to read everything and sign it. Like I told you this morning, we're here to protect you and ask you questions about a case to which you may be connected."

"Okay." I don't get it. I'm just a clueless teenager—I wouldn't know about anything. But whatever.

"Firstly: your full name is Elvira Margaret Thyme. Elvira, E-l-v-i-r-a. Thyme, T-h-y-m-e."

"Yes."

"DOB 03-21-04."

"Yes."

"Daughter of the late Louis and Katherine Thyme."

"Yes."

"What's your home address?"

I give it to him from memory, ignoring the fact that I haven't been at "home" since before my parents died in the crash. It suddenly strikes me that no one's been there to feed my cat, Ginger.

"What's your phone number? You have it with you, am I correct?" The battery is dead, but I give him the number anyway.

"Do you have any ID with you?"

"I've got my license with me." I pass it to him after fumbling around in my purse to find it. Somehow the bag has stayed with me since the crash. He looks at the card for a minute, then hands it back.

"You're a U.S. citizen."

"Yes."

"Are you currently employed?"

I hesitate for a minute. "Sort of. I got accepted for a job, but…it hasn't started yet."

"Where? And why is that?"

"Dr. Lakin's office. I applied as secretary. I haven't been able to start work yet because my background check results never came back."

"We may have to detain you for a few days for safety reasons. *Your* safety." He looks up from the paper at me. "Do you have any known allergies or medical conditions? Are you taking any medications?"

I stop to think for a minute. "I'm allergic to tree nuts. I have had eczema problems before. And no medications."

He pauses, biting his lip. "Is there anyone related to you that we need to contact about your situation?"

Suddenly my eyes tear up and I close them tightly. The aching pain in my chest is back.

Mom… Dad…

"No one," I manage to say after a moment. "My parents…were the only living relations I know about."

"I'm sorry for your loss, Miss Thyme." I can tell he means it. "Last question. Have you ever been arrested before?"

Does that imply I'm being arrested *now?*

"No."

"Alright." The agent takes a couple of papers out of his folder and snaps them to a clipboard. He hands them to me with a pen. "Can you read this over and then sign it for me?"

It takes me over five minutes in my present state, but I manage to do it. By the end, I'm not so nervous anymore, though I really want to know what I'm going to be asked about. Obviously someone tried to kill me last night, but… The police showed up so quickly that they must have already been on the way.

But why?

My right shoulder hurts a bit as I sign my name, but then it's done. I hand the papers back to the agent and he replaces them in his folder.

"Now." Suddenly his expression becomes more brisk. "Can you tell me everything that happened this morning? You said someone tried to kill you. The window of your room has been smashed, and we found three bullets in the wall. The camera shows that it was a tall, cloaked figure who shot the bullets. The shooting was soundless. Is there any other information you can give us?"

"I tried to call for help," I remember. "There wasn't really an answer. Someone just said 'Really?' And after the woman fired at me, she said 'I don't understand!'" I pause.

"So it was a woman. Did you see her face?"

I shake my head. "No."

"You were shot in the shoulder. Besides that, you were in a car accident yesterday. How are you feeling physically?"

I frown. "Wiped out."

"We can take you back to the hospital, but we don't think it's safe. Are you okay if we help you feel better while keeping you safe here?" Strangely enough, the agent actually seems concerned for me, and that's comforting.

"Where is 'here'?" I ask after a moment's thought.

The agent smiles slightly. "That's classified. But there's nowhere safer in the United States."

"Alright."

I guess I have no other choice, anyway, if I want to keep living. I have no relatives…no anything. At least they'll feed me here…I'm guessing. A slight rumble from my stomach reminds me that I haven't had breakfast yet.

"Now, Elvira Thyme, I'm going to be very official. You're being detained for your own safety and for questioning concerning a very important case. You can stop talking at any time, and whatever you say may be brought up in a court of law. Do you understand that?"

2

I nod slowly. Miranda rights. I just wish I knew why…what…

"Can you tell me exactly *what* happened in that hospital room? Every detail that you remember, in the order that you remember it."

I tell him slowly, carefully. I don't know what the deal is, but I don't want to get into trouble for something I forget now and remember later. It takes quite a few minutes, but at the end of the tale, I'm relieved. The agent seems happy with what I've told him, and doesn't ask any more about that.

However, his next question kind of blots out any relief I was feeling just now. "Have you ever heard of the Slayer?"

"No?" Never—but the way he says it sends a chill up my spine.

Agent Dola takes a deep breath before he continues. "The Slayer is a serial killer. He's been active for the past fifteen years, killing people with a silent-firing gun. He fires from empty office buildings at night. The targets are seemingly random, and the only clue we've picked up is a single fingerprint on a bullet shell dropped on a crime scene nine years ago. We've been calling him the Slayer because that was engraved on the bullet shell. It could be one person or an entire group; our only connection for all the murder cases is the method of the killing. Elvira Thyme, there are two things we need to hear your evidence about. The first is that…"

He looks closely at me. "Elvira Thyme, you had your fingerprints taken recently. The fingerprint on the bullet shell we found matches your right index finger."

…

What?

My fingerprint…connected to a serial killer?

I can feel the blood draining from my face. "I…I don't get it… *My* fingerprint?"

Nine years ago.

That means…

"But…I was nine…"

"Yes." His dark eyes are hard. "That's why we took you in for questioning… instead of arresting you on the spot. It's a serious case, Elvira. Very serious. And you are our only lead."

"Me?" This makes no sense. Way to double the confusion… I'm starting to get an actual headache. What?

He leans towards me. "Somehow, the Slayer has had access to your fingerprints. That's the only reasonable conclusion we can get from that evidence, since yes, you were nine years old. *But*, now that the Slayer has tried to kill you, we can deduce that he believes you can help us figure out his identity."

I say nothing. There's nothing to say. I know nothing about any "Slayer." I don't know anyone who would kill people like that. I don't know anyone who's even a good shot—except my dad, and he'd never have killed anyone. *I* don't remember anything important from when I was nine. How…how am I supposed to be helpful?

I shake my head dizzily. "Sorry, sir. I honestly can't help you. I have no idea what this is all about."

Suddenly the tears start to my eyes again. "I don't…I don't… Why? Why me?"

Maybe it doesn't make sense, but I can tell that the agent understands. He understands that I'm talking about not just this crazy case, but my parents… the crash…the attempted murder…

Why me? I'm only eighteen. And all this has happened overnight.

Wait, so I'm a suspect in a serial killer case? The *police* want me, too? Not just an assassin—*me?*

I'm crying now, and I can't stop.

"I'll go get some tissues," the secretary murmurs, and she leaves the room. "Elvira."

I look up at the agent. His face is filled with genuine concern.

"Elvira, I'm your friend, and I want to help you, okay?"

"Okay," I sob, holding my arms closely to my chest. It hurts…my heart hurts…

"My name is Pietro Dola, and I'm not just an FBI agent. I'm a human being and I care about you just as I would any other person. I care more about you because you're a teenager whose life looks dark right now and I'm the only one who can help you. And Elvira, I *do* want to help. I know everything looks dark right now—*really* dark—but if you're innocent, and you cooperate with us, it doesn't have to be that way."

"I don't know anything," I cry, the words tearing my throat. *"Anything!"*

"That's okay," he says, and I open my eyes to stare at him. "Just let me help you. That's all."

"What do you want me to do, sir?" I ask, confused.

"I want you to heal and to feel safe and cared for." He stands up. "There'll be a doctor here in a few minutes to see you… We want to keep you here for now so that we know you're safe, but don't feel that you're a prisoner, Elvira. You're a treasured, upright, young citizen of our country. I'll come back later today to visit you. And tomorrow…"

He smiles. "I think Lucie wants to visit you, too."

"Lucie?" How does *he* know about Lucie? But of course, the FBI has to know everything.

Suddenly a bit of color steals into his face. "This isn't work information, but… We're going to be engaged. And Lucie cares about you a lot."

He steps over to me and shakes my hand. "Thank you, Elvira. I hope we'll get to know each other better soon, and in better circumstances. And don't forget: I'm at your service, Miss Thyme."

"Thank you." The words seems strangely inadequate.

He smiles and leaves the room as the secretary comes back with a box of tissues. "Here you go, honey. Can I get you anything for breakfast before the doctor comes?"

* * *

It's a couple of days before Lucie can visit me, but when she does come, she brings a couple of large shopping bags with her.

"Good morning, Elvira," she greets me happily, shutting the door behind her. "Hey, this place is nice!"

I moved to a small "suite" type affair later that first day. It's still in the same building—wherever the building is, I don't know—but it's a bedroom, a bathroom, and something between a study and a kitchen. I'm alone a lot of the time, though Pietro has visited me each day, and the workers come to check on me and bring me meals. My phone works, but they've asked me not to contact anyone, telling me that they'll take talk to anyone who's worried about me. The solitude is sort of nice—I have helpful books and I can journal a lot to help stabilize.

And now that Lucie is visiting, things just got a whole lot better. Probably as good as things are going to get.

"It is," I smile shyly.

"How are you feeling? Is this solitary confinement, or what's the deal?" Lucie laughs, walking over to the window and opening the blinds. Sunlight floods in and immediately the room is full of light.

"I'm feeling better, actually," I say, and realize it's true. "Thank you…for coming to visit me."

It sounds awkward. But it's all I can do…and Lucie is a true friend.

"Of course." Lucie picks up her bags again and sets them on the sofa. "Okay, so, I've brought some things for you… Clothes, books, snacks, and a card game."

She winks. "I brought my favorite game, because incidentally, I'm going to be the one playing it with you today. I hope you like it, too. As well as everything else, of course." She looks at me. "Well, what are you waiting for?"

I reach into the first bag and pull out a pink hoodie. It's got *Stronger than the Storm* written on the back. I laugh. This is so like me…the me I used to be, anyway.

She's brought me some more casual wear, and a dice game, and a notebook, and a couple of young adult novels. As well as some snacks and gum. I'm busy trying to think of the best way to express my thanks, when she reaches into her purse.

"I brought something else, too," she says more seriously, "but I don't know if…"

Suddenly she seems to make up her mind and pulls out an *Imitation of Christ*. "Would you care to have this?"

"Yes, please!" My jaw drops as I realize she must be Catholic, too. She wears skirts…I wonder…

"I'm a Traditional Catholic," she smiles. "And if you know what that means, you know everyth—"

She breaks off suddenly as I throw my arms around her.

"Thank you so much," I tell her. "Thank you. *Thank you.*"

Her face is alight with smiles. "I'm just glad I can help you…and delighted to meet another Traditionalist. That makes me happy. You're on the right track, Elvira. You're going to be okay."

3

"Y ou can't deny that Miss Thyme is innocent of any crime attributed to the Slayer. Her background is clean except for the one fingerprint, which was lifted when she was nine years old. We haven't got enough evidence to arrest her, let alone put her on trial."

FBI Agent Pietro Dola was angry.

He was *very* angry. The other authorities on the case wanted to try Elvira for the serial murders. To Pietro, the idea was ridiculous. It shouldn't have even been suggested. "But we have nothing else to work with," someone argued. Officer Farren. "Thyme is our only lead. Plus, it is easily apparent that the Slayer wants her dead. She *must* have some information, information that *you* have failed to get from her."

He glared at the young, "upstart" agent. He didn't believe in Pietro's simple, considerate practice. He believed that the culprit had to be found, as soon as possible, and punished. Before anyone else was killed. The most recent Slayer killing—apart from the attempt on Elvira's life—had been only three months ago.

"I think we need to keep trying. Maybe a trial will scare her."

"We've gotten every proof of truth from her." Pietro shook his head. "We've used a lie detector and muscle testing. She is clear of intentional falsehood. No, you can't do that to an innocent teenager. Besides which, a public trial would mean putting her life in danger. It'd also blot her record forever."

One of Officer Farren's colleagues, Officer Rivera, scowled. "You don't understand, *Agent Dola*." Pietro restrained a wince at the attempt to pull rank. "This is a serious case and it calls for serious measures. There are four reasons why Thyme needs to be put on trial. Firstly, it will force the Slayer to take action, whether the Slayer is a group or a person. It will also prove Thyme's innocence...or guilt.

"Secondly, as I mentioned, the situation is exceptional. We need to solve this case, even if it means potential risk for a single person. We're here to protect the general public.

"Thirdly, no one can say that Elvira is unconnected to the case, whether voluntarily or involuntarily. *The prints don't lie.*

"And lastly, now that we finally have a lead, we *have* to act on it. Otherwise, what does that say about the judicial forces in this country? It says we're incompetent and can't manage to stop a serial killer. It's bad enough already, Agent Dola. The Slayer has been laughing at us for fifteen years now."

Pietro sighed. He wasn't backing down in this case, but he was beginning to get tired of arguing.

For two weeks the FBI, the US Marshal's Service, and the USAO had been discussing the case and what to do about it. Now it had boiled down to two distinct factions. One group wanted Elvira put on public trial. The other wanted her protected and her reputation untainted.

Personally, Pietro wanted Elvira in the witness protection program, living with someone who'd look out for her. Someone who'd care for her. And he wanted it to happen soon.

Ultimately, though, he knew the decision wasn't his to make. It would be the Attorney General of the Criminal Division.

Pietro was still going to fight for Elvira.

"My points still stand," he said simply. "We've been throwing the same stones at each other for the past two weeks. I'm not going to pull out a thesaurus to find a new way to put it. No, it's time for us to stop arguing. I've made my presentation; you can all look back at it if you like. Whatever you say isn't going to change my mind."

He stood up, pushed his chair back in, and left the room, taking his briefcase with him. It took him a only few minutes to get down to the front lobby. He logged out on a wall tablet.

"Going home so soon, Agent?" the pretty young receptionist asked.

Pietro smiled absently. "Yes."

"We'll see you tomorrow?"

"No." Pietro smiled to himself. Tomorrow...would be one of the most important days in his life.

As he got into his car, he grinned. He didn't usually leave work this early, but now he'd have time to visit Elvira. And give her the news that he was going to be baptized tomorrow.

* * *

"How do you feel?" Lucie asked, her face bright with happiness. "I'm so, so, so happy for you!"

"Can I take you out for breakfast? Father's coming, too," Pietro told her, ignoring the fact that he felt happier than he'd ever felt in his life.

Nothing could stop him now...nothing.

"No...I'm keeping an empty time slot because I'm hoping someone will ask me out." Lucie laughed merrily as Pietro's face twisted into horror. "And he just did! Yes, I'll be happy to have breakfast with you and Father."

Pietro's face was wreathed in smiles as he got into his car. Everything was perfect.

No...there could only be one more perfect.

Everything *else* was great, though. Pietro shoved his FBI work into the back corner of his mind and left it there. He wasn't going to let it bother him today.

"Father's going to meet us at Collins," he told Lucie, answering her inquiring glance. "He said he has something he has to do quickly before he comes."

"Sounds good," she smiled, slipping into the passenger seat.

"How's work been? You took today off, didn't you?" Pietro asked as he started the car and drove out of the small mission chapel parking lot.

"It's been okay... I've had a lot of night shifts lately. I think one of our nurses stopped working. Other than that, everything's been pretty normal."

Lucie sighed. She knew better than to ask Pietro about Elvira's case, but she was dying to know what was happening.

"I've been wanting to ask you out for dinner sometime... Do you think next Friday would work?" Pietro cast a careful sideways glance at Lucie.

"Let me see..." Lucie pulled out her phone and checked her calendar. "Yes, as far as I know. Where? What time?"

"Wherever is your favorite place in the whole world," Pietro told her simply. It might have sounded cliché, but he meant it. "Probably six in the afternoon. I can drive you, too."

"Sounds awesome. I'll have to figure out my favorite place, though," Lucie laughed.

"Thank you," Pietro said, and Lucie stared at him.

"Thank you?"

"Thank you for being a part of my life."

Lucie didn't answer as Pietro pulled towards the curb and parked. Lucie smiled and thanked him as he got out first and whipped around the car to open the door for her.

"Now, don't forget, I'm paying," he insisted as they walked in the door of the small café together.

"Alright, fine," Lucie sighed.

"Next time, too. —Huh?" Pietro's sentence was cut short as his phone began to ring. He pulled it out, confused; he'd silenced it.

The name of the caller told him everything. It was the Attorney General of the Criminal Division.

"Sorry, sorry, I have to take this," Pietro told Lucie, and she nodded understandingly. She went ahead to find a table, and he ducked outside, answering the call as he did so.

"'Morning, Agent Dola." Richard Lance's voice was unmistakable to anyone who worked under him. "Are you able to discuss anything right now?"

"Yes, sir," Pietro answered. Oh, if only it was about Elvira...and good news...

He wasn't wrong—about the first part, anyway. "The decision about the Thyme case was finalized this morning, Agent Dola. I understand you're Thyme's strongest supporter?"

"Yes, sir, I am." Pietro swallowed hard.

"Then I'd like to inform you that Thyme is going to be placed in our witness protection program."

Yes, Pietro thought to himself—and then stopped smiling as the Attorney General continued.

"However, that'll be after a couple of months of intense security containment and further questioning. Is that clear? This decision is not to be contested."

"Very clear, sir." Pietro bit his lip like the hot-headed Italian-American he was. "I assume I am still affiliated with her case?"

"You are—you're her chief defendant. However, of course you know that only high-ranking officials will be allowed to see and speak with her. That includes you, Agent Dola, but it doesn't include your girlfriend."

Pietro winced. Richard couldn't have put it any more plainly.

"But of course," he answered smoothly, though he was seething inside at the obvious reference to Lucie. "Is there anything else, sir?"

"No. Thank you, Agent Dola."

"Thank you, sir. Goodbye."

Pietro hung up, and stood still for a moment on the sidewalk. He had to process for a minute.

Elvira was going to be intensely questioned, while living a practically solitary life, for two months. Then she'd be released as a citizen, but

with a new name and totally new surroundings. The thought stung
Pietro.

Elvira...she was already emotionally and mentally traumatized. What
would *this* do to her? It was almost as bad as being put on trial. At least
she'd be protected from the Slayer, but still...

Pietro sighed, again shoving the case to the back of his mind as Father
Cyprian came walking up. "You waited for me!"

"Of course, Father. Lucie—Miss Bernard—is inside. We're glad you
could join us."

"It's very nice to go out to breakfast with the two of you." Father
Cyprian smiled as Pietro held the café door open for him.

"Yes... Oh, and Father, I'm paying." Pietro smiled back.

* * *

I'm sitting on the armchair in the "living room," reading a book, when I get
the call. It's from a number I don't recognize, but then a name shows up
underneath and I realize it's from one of the high-up authorities. I answer it,
a bit scared. It must have to do with the decision they've been trying to make
about me... I breathe the Holy Names. Oh, please let it be good news!

"Elvira Thyme?"

"Yes, that's me." I don't recognize the voice at all.

"Hello, Miss Thyme. I am Richard Lance, Attorney General. Could I meet
with you in a few minutes? At ten o'clock, to be exact?"

"Y—yes." I swallow hard. I don't know what Attorney General means, but
it sure sounds important. "Um, where—"

"I'll have someone show you to my office."

Oh. So he's actually in the building right now. Well, it's nice of him to call
and ask me before sending for me, I guess.

"Okay."

"I look forward to meeting you, Miss Thyme. I've heard a lot about you."

I blink a couple of times. "Thank you, sir."

He hangs up, and I look at the time. 9:52.

I'm dressed pretty casually, but it'll have to be okay. I have only three outfits anyway. It's not like I go anywhere special. At least I can wear skirts. That's a plus.

I can feel my breathing becoming shallower and shallower. I guess it's probably just the built-up tension. I try to reason with myself, but myself simply doesn't listen. By the time someone knocks on the door three minutes later, I'm so tense I'm almost faint. My skin is clammy.

"Good morning, Miss Thyme," the woman smiles. I try to smile back and fail miserably.

"Right this way," she directs me.

It takes us a few minutes to go up the elevator and down a hallway, but we're standing outside a door and the woman is knocking at 10:00, sharp. She opens it and holds it open. I realize in shock that she wants me to go in first. I step into the office, and the door is closed behind me.

It's just a normal office. The man behind the desk gestures for me to sit down.

"Hello, Miss Thyme." He holds out his hand across the desk, and I shake it after a moment of hesitation. "Thank you for coming to see me this morning."

"Is it bad news, sir?" I ask, annoyed that my voice is so trembly.

"Well, it depends on what you'd consider bad news." He smiles, but doesn't laugh. I'm grateful for that. "You're not going to be arrested or put on trial."

I breathe a sigh of intense relief.

"But," he goes on, "we *will* ask you to cooperate for a couple of months of close security. You're important to us, Miss Thyme. Someone tried to break into this building last night. We're going to move you to a more undercover place. Somewhere where we will be absolutely sure of your safety.

"During that time, we'll try to see if you can remember anything that will help us in our search for the *Slayer*. Your cooperation will be greatly appreciated. After we believe it safe, we'll put you into the Witness Protection Program. You won't have to worry."

His smile drops. "I know you've had a crazy last month. I am truly sorry for everything you've endured. But this is only temporary, Miss Thyme. We hope that after rehab you will be able to lead a normal life. We want the best for you, and we hope you realize that."

Confinement and then identity erasure. I get it… My body doesn't relax; it just gets more tense, if that's even possible. I realize dimly that I am about to burst into tears.

"Miss Thyme? Do you want to—" Richard's question is cut short as I cover my face with my hands.

The tears spill through my fingers. I am so mad at myself…such a display of emotion…this man must despise me.

But I can't help it.

"Miss Thyme!"

"I'm sorry," I gasp out. "I…I don't understand…I want to go home, I just want to go home!"

4

I've been here a week and a half now. I've seen no one except a couple of officers who've come to ask me questions, and one woman who brings me meals. I have no contact with the outside world. There are no sunny windows…only cold walls that seem to laugh when I try to imagine pictures there. The *Imitation* is the only book they've left me. Plus a NIV "Bible." There's no way I am going to touch that thing.

Slowly, I feel that I'm falling apart more and more. God seems so far away, even though I know He isn't. I haven't been to Mass in weeks. Lucie is gone. Agent Dola hasn't come, either. They've just…deserted me, I guess. And even though I know God deserts no one, I still feel it. My mom used to tell me that feelings aren't always accurate, and I remind myself of that. But I'm very far from the strong woman I would like to be…someone who'd not be crushed by everything that's happening. Someone who'd not break down in front of police officials.

But I'm just Elvira Thyme. Helpless and afraid.

Someone knocks on the door. I jump up from the couch. The woman with the food never knocks.

The door opens slowly, and my jaw drops in happy surprise as I see it's none other than…the agent.

"Good afternoon, Miss Thyme," he greets me. "How are you doing?"

"I'm—I'm—I'm happy to see you." I struggle to find the most optimistic truth. "You—you came?"

"Well, I'm here, aren't I?" The agent looks shocked as I hug him suddenly.

"Whoa. Sit down." He's never given me such a direct command before. "Why are you so worked up—"

"Worked up" is an understatement. I burst into tears as I step away.

"Okay, okay." He's never looked so disturbed. "Uh—sit down, will you? There. And, um, I brought chocolate for you."

He hands me a chocolate bar, but it's not chocolate I want. I want answers, and I want help.

"Agent Dola, I don't know if you can do anything, but—"

He's quickly recovering from his surprise, and now he points at the chocolate. "Eat that...please. And you can call me Pietro. Okay. What?"

"I can't stay here, Pietro." I've stopped crying, now, but my voice is still choked. "I can't!"

"It's only two months." Pietro bites his lip. "And then—"

"And then I'll never see you again, or Lucie, or be allowed to talk to you, and I'll probably have to stay with someone who's not even Catholic, and I don't know where they're going to send me, and—!" All my fears come rushing out all at once. "*How?* What do I do? And they keep questioning me, and I don't know anything! I've told them *everything!* I'd rather be—" I don't finish the sentence, because I *will* it not to be true.

But I feel it. Horribly strongly.

"Listen, Elvira, I need you to calm down, okay?" Pietro tells me. "Breathe. *Breathe!*"

I close my eyes, focusing on breathing. I feel him hand me a tissue, and I dry my face.

"That's better." Pietro sounds relieved, and I open my eyes. "Keep breathing."

"Okay."

"Now, are you okay *right now?* Ignore the future," Pietro asks a couple of minutes later. "Just think about the present."

"I guess." I have to think for a moment. "I have food, water, a place to sleep, clothes, heat."

That's actually pretty good, I realize. I've just had it easy.

"Now, you're pretty well off, Elvira." Pietro sounds a bit like he's trying to reason with a five-year-old, but that's okay. "What do you do all day?"

"Nothing." There's bitterness in my voice. "Nothing, unless they want to talk to me. And they've only done that twice in the past week."

"Hmm." Pietro pulls a deck of cards out of his pocket. "Do you know how to play cards?"

* * *

"Father, what do I do?" Pietro finished. His face was tight. "Elvira can't handle this kind of stress after all she's been through. But the officials won't budge. There are people in the network that don't care about Elvira as a person. They just want the case closed. Meanwhile Elvira is getting deeply depressed. I'm just surprised she hasn't fully snapped yet. But it's only a matter of time. This treatment is designed to break professionals. But she can't help us broken!"

His voice trembled. "Father, it's *wrong!* But if I do anything, Elvira will be mistreated. It might get even worse."

Father Cyprian sighed and was silent for a moment.

"You have to act according to your conscience. I can't tell you what to do in circumstances like these. You'll have to pray about it. Consider your duties to God...and to your neighbor."

Pietro bit his lip.

"Thank you, Father."

* * *

"Lucie, I want to talk seriously to you tonight," Pietro told her after they ordered their food, the Friday night he'd asked her to join him for dinner. "Not like I'm not always serious. But tonight especially."

"Alright." Lucie smiled. "That's why you wanted to sit outside. I see."

Pietro nodded approvingly. "Right. You're getting good!"

The young woman laughed. "What's on your mind, Pietro?"

30

"Lucie…" Pietro bit his lip as his mind went blank.

Lucie's voice softened as she leaned forward. "Is something wrong?"

"Oh, *dai*," Pietro muttered. He took a deep breath and slipped off his chair, onto his knees. He pulled a small box out of his pocket. "Miss Bernard, I'm not a perfect man. I—I didn't grow up like you did. I've got a lot to learn before I can come *close* to anyone that could be worthy of you. But, Lucie, I want to try—if you will let me. Miss Lucie Bernard, will you marry me?"

Lucie caught her breath in surprise. A lone tear sparkled in her eyes and ran down her cheek.

Pietro froze in horror. "Are those—are those happy tears?"

"The happiest." Lucie smiled through her tears. "Pietro, yes, yes, yes. Absolutely yes. I…I was *hoping* you'd ask, Pietro." She looked down and saw his olive-toned hands shaking with the box. Pietro managed to open it, and she gave him her hand. He was shaking too hard, so she helped him slip the engagement ring onto her finger. Lucie looked up, and Pietro was crying too. The happiest tears.

"Good heavens," she laughed weakly. "Pietro…*thank you*."

* * *

"Miss Thyme, our conversation is over for now, but it will be continued." The man stands up, walks out the door, and shuts and locks it behind him. I collapse back onto the couch. The tears that I've been holding back for the past half hour come pouring out. I'm sure they've got it on camera, but I don't care. I'm done. I'm done. I can't take any more of this.

Why can't they just leave me alone?

Now they want me to lie. To say I know something. To make the Slayer desperate.

But I *don't* know anything. That's the truth, and they just don't seem to get it. I don't know *anything!*

A scream cuts from my throat. I bury my face in the cushion, sobbing. I'm a mess, but it doesn't matter. No one is going to come see me, anyway. No one.

No one!

"Oh God, help me," I cry, the words muffled by the cushion. "Help me…help me…"

There is no answer, only silence. I grab my rosary from my pocket and begin to murmur *Hail Marys.*

But it all seems so empty. So meaningless.

"No, it's not," I scream into the quiet. "I *know* You're there! You *have* to be!"

* * *

"Yes, she'll snap in a few days and say whatever we want her to say." The voice was loud and confident, and it caught Pietro's attention. He froze.

"Good. Then we'll release it to the press, and the Slayer will have no choice but to finish this. Obviously, we'll be waiting. The Slayer won't stand a chance—"

Pietro finished pulling the folder out of his locker. On second thought, he replaced it in his briefcase and took the whole case out. Leaving his locker empty and locked, he headed outside to his car. His brain was working fast.

So that was the new plan, the plan he hadn't been told about. Elvira was only good as bait now. The thought filled him with anger at the corruption of the law force that he was only now beginning to see and recognize. Pietro had recognized one of the voices to belong to Officer Rivera. Of course. Now that they'd partially won their case, they weren't going to give up. They'd catch the Slayer.

Even if it meant risking Elvira's life.

These men had no idea whom they were dealing with, Pietro told himself. The Slayer? No one had ever seen them, except Elvira. The Slayer's weapons were like nothing that they'd dealt with before. How did they know what they were getting themselves into? Elvira could easily be killed.

Plus, they were trying to break her. In itself, that was bad enough.

Pietro tossed his briefcase onto the passenger seat of his car, then slipped into his driver's seat and caught his breath as he saw the gun in the rearview mirror. He usually checked his car before he got into it, but this time...

"Hands up, officer." The voice was strangely familiar, but Pietro didn't have time to figure it out now.

Neatly rolling from his driver's seat out the door, Pietro slipped under his car and hit an emergency button on his belt. He was still just outside the facility. Backup wouldn't take long to arrive.

Some glass from the windshield hit the pavement past his head. But there'd been no crashing sound, no gunshot. Pietro realized he was dealing with none other than the famous Slayer, and he bit his lip. No one had escaped from the Slayer alive...except Elvira...and hopefully himself.

His mind worked fast. The Slayer would be out of the car in an instant. Pietro wouldn't stand a chance. He could shoot at legs, but he didn't know what weapons the Slayer was carrying or what protective equipment they had. If Pietro wanted to live, he had one option.

He wasn't going to let it end here. Not this way.

Besides which, he had some extremely important papers on the passenger seat of his car. Pietro began rolling away from the car, pulling out his handgun as he did so. He shot the gas line underneath the car twice, then curled up into a tight ball and held his breath as he rolled.

It was only a few seconds before the car exploded, but it seemed like an eternity to Pietro. His jacket caught fire, but he kept rolling and escaped with some minor burns. He didn't appreciate the fact that half his jacket and a bit of his shirt was gone as well.

Pietro stood up and surveyed the burning vehicle. His papers were still there, but the briefcase was fireproof. He'd be able to get them back after a bomb squad or whatever examined the whole situation.

Pietro stared almost vacantly into the flames. Sirens were screaming and people were rushing out of the building, but the man was distracted by something else.

No one had run away from or been thrown out of the car. That meant the Slayer had to be inside.

Had Pietro...

Had Pietro killed the Slayer?

24 May 2021

0946

Time Loop: 1102-1108 Notes: Failure

24 May 2021

Notes: Failure

25 May 2021

Travel: present

17 October 2104

1202

Logged Off

Username:

Passcode:

Logged On

Travel: 30 May 2021 1900

Logged Off

"Sorry, Agent Dola, but no one is to be granted access to Miss Thyme." The receptionist's tone was hard and final. Pietro frowned. "Here's my ID. My status is—"

"I'm afraid your status isn't enough, Agent." The woman's eyes were steely today. "Please leave the facility."

Pietro realized with a burst of shock that the woman had been

specially told to refuse him. He nodded and walked away.

He didn't leave, though. He headed for the kitchen.

***Need some breakfast.* Pietro grinned to himself.**

* * *

Breakfast is a muffin, some yogurt, and some fruit, as usual. I suddenly notice a capsule in the fruit, and frown. What, are they trying to *drug* me now?

Then I realize that the capsule isn't filled with powder…but paper instead. It's a very thin strip, but it's readable. Just a bunch of dots and dashes. I resist a giggle.

When exactly did I tell Pietro I learned Morse code for fun? After the dots and dashes is his signature.

Trust me and eat your yogurt quickly. Put anything important to you in your pocket. No phone. Pietro.

I'm confused, but…

Okay.

I trust him. Whatever he's planning, I trust him.

The yogurt tastes disgusting, but I force it down, as quickly as I can. Obviously Pietro added something to it. I grab my *Imitation* and put it into my pocket, and then a thought hits me. If I don't finish all of my breakfast, and wash out the yogurt container, Pietro will be caught in whatever he's trying to do. I finish the fruit and am halfway through the muffin when…a wave of nausea hits me.

What…okay.

I stumble to the bathroom and rinse out the yogurt container, throwing it away. Then I lose control and throw up…into the garbage can, on top of the yogurt container.

Was *that* what Pietro wanted? I'm confused…

I'm okay for now. I walk back to the "living room" and sit down on the couch before picking up the muffin to attempt to finish it.

The blackness hits me like a bullet and I slump over on the couch.

***

"Lucie, are you on a night shift tonight? Please tell me you are."

Lucie was confused. It wasn't often that Pietro began a phone call with that kind of line.

"I mean, I am. Why? Are you hurt?"

"Can you meet me at the park and leave your phone in the car? I have to talk to you about something extremely important."

Maybe Pietro was just a pessimist because he was a secret agent, but Lucie decided she'd play along for his sake. "Alright. I'll see you there. When?"

"As soon as you possibly can."

"Okay. Goodbye. See you soon."

Lucie stared at her phone as Pietro hung up.

She finished the last bite of her breakfast burrito, then locked her apartment door and went outside. The park was only a five minute's drive away. But Lucie's thoughts were very busy as she drove. What could Pietro possibly need from her?

She smiled at the engagement ring on her finger. Whatever it was, she was going to do her best.

Pietro was waiting for her, she realized as she parked. She slid her phone under the seat and got out of the car.

"Over here!" Pietro waved, and Lucie waved back, though she'd already seen him.

"Okay. What are we doing?" she asked him once she'd walked closer.

"Let's walk the trail loop." Pietro was obviously preoccupied. "Thank you for coming, Lucie."

"But of course," she answered, then went silent. Pietro would tell her when he was ready.

"Lucie, you have a choice. I'm not going to force you into anything." Pietro bit his lip as he walked quickly—a bit too quickly for Lucie. She struggled to keep up with him. "Lucie, I have to do something... something hard and dangerous. It's up to you if you want to help me.

I'm going to become a dangerous man to be around, Lucie. I don't want to force that on you, so I'm going to be open with you."

"Okay. Can we slow down a bit?"

"I'm sorry. Yes." Pietro flushed as he slowed his pace drastically. "So... Lucie, it's up to you. Are you willing to be engaged to..."

"Look, I know you, and I know your morals. Whatever danger you're getting yourself into is a *just* danger, Pietro. And of course I'm willing to share it with you."

Pietro looked at her. "Even if it means going off the radar?"

Lucie caught her breath for a moment before she answered.

"Even if it means going off the radar. I haven't got any family who'd care."

"Even if it means leaving the country?"

He watched her face.

Lucie's voice was firm. "Even if it means leaving the country, Pietro, so long as you're there to manage it. I'm helping you, and that's my answer. Now, what do you need me to do?"

"It's about Elvira," Pietro confided, and Lucie's jaw dropped. "They're going to use her to find a criminal, and that's not right. Lucie, I'm going to get her out."

"Isn't she in one of the most secure—" Lucie was shocked. "How? How are you going to do that?"

"See, the place she's in doesn't have high-quality medical care." Pietro smiled suddenly. "Actually, she's not there anymore. If everything is going according to plan, she's on her way to the hospital right now."

"What happened? Is she okay?" Lucie gasped.

"She's fine," Pietro laughed. "She'll just be unconscious for the next eighteen hours. Unconscious, with low blood pressure, low oxygen. They'll have her in intensive care. She'll recover around five in the morning. At that point, Lucie, I'm going to rely on you to smuggle her outside. I've got papers for you and for her. I know you can do it."

Lucie was having a bit of brain trouble. "You want me to smuggle a highly wanted informant under police guard out of a hospital?"

"If you're willing to do it," Pietro hesitated.

"Sounds good." Lucie surprised even herself by the confidence in her voice. "What happens after that?"

Pietro bit his lip. "Lucie, this is going to sound crazy, but..."

"Fire away. It can't get any more crazy." Lucie laughed.

"She needs to stay with someone I can trust implicitly. Only overnight. Then we'll have to move her."

"I...see." Lucie smiled. "Well, you've got it."

"I can pick her up and take her to your place and wait there," Pietro went on. "See, this is going to have to be a private Witness Protection program. I'm going to have Elvira change her name, her looks, etc. I have someone I can trust helping me. If it comes down to it, she'll be able to leave the country with her new papers. I already have some from my work. You shouldn't need any, but if you do, I know where to get them."

Lucie shook her head to try to get rid of the distinct feeling of unreality. What was she *doing?*

She was becoming an accomplice to breaking out a highly wanted suspect. Was this a bad idea? She had to think this over...logically...

Rescuing someone from injustice was definitely within her moral code, she decided. Even if it meant endangering herself... But Pietro could do it. He'd been an FBI for years. He'd worked on several top secret cases. He knew the system and the law like the back of his hand.

"What happens after that?" Lucie asked. "Is it for sure that we're going to leave the country?"

"No. I'm hoping to talk to someone soon who can fix the situation for us. What they're doing to Elvira isn't right. We just have to make that public, and they'll have no chance but to back down. In the meantime, we have to protect Elvira from...someone who's trying to kill her."

He sighed. "Okay, I've already told you too much, so you may as well know all. Lucie, there's a serial killer who considers Elvira a loose end, though she doesn't know why. The serial killer framed Elvira with a single fingerprint. That's why she was taken in for questioning. We can't get any information out of her. But the Slayer—that's what we call the killer—is still trying to kill her. I was attacked just this morning, outside the facility. It's not safe for Elvira there."

"*You* were attacked?" Lucie stared at him, a new fear in her eyes.

Pietro nodded, trying not to overemphasize his experience. "I...I actually don't know what to think about it. I blew up my car with the Slayer inside. But...no traces were found."

A chill ran down Lucie's spine. "No...traces?"

"Nothing. There was nobody in the car."

"Then—"

Pietro sighed. "I know. I've told them ten times what I saw and heard. A gun and a threat. I don't think they actually believe me. That's just another reason why I'm going off the radar. Lucie, I think I'm under suspicion, too. I've shown too much support for Elvira, and now this has happened. I wasn't allowed to go see her today. They're cutting me off. That's why I'm acting now. Besides the fact that Elvira is..." He broke off.

"What?" Lucie looked at him. "Elvira is what?"

Pietro scowled. "Elvira has been stretched to the point of snapping."

Lucie was quiet for a moment, and then she stopped walking and looked earnestly at Pietro. Her face was tight.

"I will do whatever we have to do to help her," she promised. "I'm with you. You can count on me."

5

Pietro scowled as he was told that his briefcase was being held for inspection. He knew what that meant. They were confiscating his papers. But he needed them, and he didn't have time to go through the legal loops.

By the time he left the facility for the last time, his folder of papers for Elvira's case was tucked safely under his arm. He wasn't going to risk his careful research being destroyed. That research was his hope for Elvira's public redemption. Dusk was falling. Pietro got into his car and began driving. In the back seat were a couple of grocery bags with girls' clothing, hair dye, chocolate...and a bouquet of flowers. Next to them was a stuffed wallet and a passport, both tucked into the front pocket of a new, girly backpack.

As Pietro drove to the hospital, he went over the plans once more.

Elvira was in a carefully protected section of the hospital. Lucie was going to smuggle her out. There was no way they could cover that up, but Pietro was hoping that once Elvira was cleared, Lucie's reputation would be saved.

She'd get the drowsy Elvira out to the car Pietro had rented with his fake name. They'd all drive to Lucie's place. Elvira would stay there overnight, and a few hours later, Pietro would pick her and Lucie up. They'd go to the city park, from whence a helicopter would take them to a little clearing in the woods. From there, Pietro knew where to go. He had many influential friends. One, Stan Weber, was a propaganda expert. Pietro had called him earlier, and Stan was ready and waiting to help them. He was a good guy.

He was also off the radar.

Pietro had had several qualms about pulling Lucie into this, but it was the only choice he had if he wanted to help Elvira. And she wanted to help Elvira, too. Besides, God was on their side. They'd be alright. Lucie was amazing. Everything would go smoothly. The Slayer would have no idea that Elvira wasn't in official custody anymore. Hopefully the cops would finally catch him.

Pietro remembered the voice he'd heard in his police car that morning. Funny...it hadn't sounded like a man's voice. Pietro was pretty sure the Slayer had to be a woman.

It was quite dark when he pulled up to a back exit of the hospital, one not many people knew about. Lucie had told him carefully where to go.

* * *

Lucie breathed a sigh of relief as she headed towards the exit, pushing Elvira's wheelchair. So far so good. She'd gotten past all the checkpoints. Now everything should go smoothly...

She opened the emergency exit door she'd carefully dewired earlier. Pushing Elvira out, she looked around for Pietro's car. He'd likely have the headlights off...

There were two cars. Someone had just closed the driver's door of one of them, and now began to walk closer. They were wearing dark clothes and a hood. Lucie couldn't make out their face. But they didn't move like Pietro.

"Pietro?" she called softly, and suddenly the truth hit her.

"Pietro! Take her!" Lucie yelled as the other car's door opened. "Now!"

Lucie grabbed the wheelchair and gave it a mighty push in the direction of Pietro's car.

"Lucie, what's—" Pietro's voice broke off as he took in the scene.

Elvira's wheelchair came crashing off the curb, and he caught the mostly unconscious teen, shoving her into the back seat of his car.

"Wha..." Elvira mumbled, coming awake slowly.

"Stay here," Pietro told her, slamming the door shut a moment later.

He turned, running, to help Lucie. His heart stopped as he saw her on the ground, with the other person bending over. Pietro pulled out his gun and shot the third party, once, twice, thrice. The shots echoed and re-echoed. The person stumbled, fell.

Lucie couldn't tell which vehicle was Pietro's, so she paused a moment, hoping he'd get out. A few seconds later, the door of one opened, and Pietro began walking over. Lucie didn't join him right away—she was studying the person in the other car. There wasn't much to see, just a hooded figure. But Lucie felt distinctly uncomfortable.

"Is something wrong?" Pietro asked her as he came up to them. He took the handles of the wheelchair.

"That car." Lucie gestured. "Let's get out of here."

"That's not a police or a hospital vehicle," Pietro noted as he began to push Elvira towards the back doors. "It's probably just an employee's, right?"

"I guess." Lucie scowled as she opened the door for him. "They shouldn't be hanging around back here, though. Oh, well. Not like we're not going to be caught anyway."

Pietro glanced at her. "I'm sorry. It's too late to go ba—"

"I know." Lucie forced a smile. "Elvira, are you awake yet?"

"Wha..." the teenager mumbled, and both eyes opened slowly. "... Lucie?"

"Let's get into the car," Lucie told her, patiently but firmly. "It's okay. Trust me."

Elvira grabbed the handle to try to stand up, and Lucie helped her collapse onto the back seat of the car. She turned, and Pietro was already pushing the wheelchair back to the curb. "Ready to go?" he called back to her.

Lucie noticed that the other car was pulling away slowly. She got the feeling that the driver was studying the license plate of Pietro's rental car.

Wordlessly, she slipped into the passenger seat, praying Pietro would come soon. Five seconds later he got into the driver's seat and started pulling away from the curb.

"That other driver is up to no good," Lucie told him. She shivered. "I can feel it. They're not friendly."

Pietro hoped she was wrong, but he knew she had good instincts. "Then let me know if we end up being followed," he told her.

"Okay. You put my suitcase in the trunk, right?"

"Right." Pietro glanced at the rearview mirror for a moment. "Elvira, are you awake?"

"Yeah. What's going on?" the teenager asked slowly.

"We're rescuing you." Lucie grinned. "Are you good with that?"

"My head hurts." Elvira seemed a bit preoccupied. "What...what was that, Pietro?"

"A classified drug I don't remember the formula for," Pietro laughed. "Sorry about the hangover."

"Where are we going?" She seemed to be coming back to life. "What... it's night already?"

"We're going to Lucie's house and you can sleep off the headache there. And then we'll go somewhere safer. Elvira, you are now doubly wanted by the state, and so are we. This is an unauthorized transfer."

Lucie had been looking behind them, and now she turned to Pietro. "Yes," she frowned. "We're being followed."

* * *

By the time we get safely to Lucie's house, it's almost five in the morning. I've dozed off a few times as Pietro tried to shake our follower, but now he's finally satisfied. I'm looking forward to "sleeping off the drug," but—

"Sorry, you two haven't got time to rest after all," Pietro apologizes as he pulls up to an apartment complex. "Elvira, we're going to dye your hair, change your clothes, you name it. Lucie will help you. I'll be back in an hour with another car, okay, Lucie? Obviously, don't answer the phone or the door. But you know that."

"Go do what you've got to do," Lucie smiles at him. "I'll take care of Elvira." She grabs the bags on the seat with me and guides me to her apartment door. I look around in delight: her little place is tastefully decorated, and I fall in love with it after having stayed over a month in what I consider solitary confinement.

"Do you like it?" Lucie fairly beams.

"I *love* it!" I tell her.

But she's already moving on to business. "Okay. Let's get a move on. I'll rub this dye into your hair, and then you can change, in case this stuff spills. Hmm, it's a bleach," she notes. "You'll have blond hair, I guess. Hope you're okay with that."

I laugh. Like I have a choice?

It doesn't take her long, and soon she's rinsing her work in her bathroom sink. My eyes are shut tightly at her request. Now she tells me to open them, and I am shocked by what I see in the mirror. Elvira Thyme is gone... In her place is a freckled, blond-haired teenager that looks strangely grown up. Lucie laughs happily.

"This is fun. Now let's get you changed!"

* * *

"Pietro has no sense of fashion," she decides a few minutes later. "Well, at least it's modest."

I nod my head, looking down at myself. I'm wearing a white T-shirt that's slightly too big for me, a long flowered skirt, and a hot pink jacket with a hoodie. Definitely not my style, but it'll do. I'm wearing this because...the other clothes he bought for me are even less normal.

I giggle. "At least I'm not going to be seen by anyone, so I don't have to worry about what I'm wearing." That's definitely a plus, even if it's slightly negative.

"Right." Lucie hands me the purse, and I slip it on. She pulls out a passport and inspects the picture.

"Well, it's not too different from how you actually look," she decides, handing it to me.

I look at it before slipping it into the purse. My name is Cassandra Bernard, apparently.

"How'd Pietro do all this?" I'm shocked. What are his plans? "And why?"

"Because you're being used and neither of us are okay with that." Lucie frowns. "It's not your fault, so don't think you're bothering us, because you aren't."

"What happens next?"

Lucie glances over at the clock. "Well, Pietro will be here in about fifteen minutes. He's going to take us somewhere and then we'll get picked up by a helicopter. After that, I don't know where we'll be going. It's probably better that we ask as few questions as possible. He knows what he's doing. I'm just helping him…and you." She smiles.

I suddenly notice the ring on her finger for the first time. "Hey, are you—"

"Yes," she beams.

I throw my arms around her. "I'm so happy for you—"

Suddenly fear seizes me, and I let go, backing away.

"What's wrong?" Lucie asks.

"You and Pietro are trashing your careers for me, aren't you?" My voice is shaky. "You're throwing away your lives…for *me*…"

"No, Elvira, it's not like that!" Lucie hugs me this time. "Pietro's got a plan, and it will work. The FBI will have to ignore your case when the public finds out what's going on. We're just protecting you for now because they aren't. Pietro and I aren't going to be affected in the long term. We're *choosing* to take this risk because we *care* about you—and because letting you be victimized is against our moral code, Elvira. You're not making us do anything, do you understand me?"

"Okay," I murmur, letting the tension go.

Lucie holds me tightly.

Mom...

Then there is knocking at the door, and all my fear comes back. I half-scream, jumping back.

Lucie doesn't lose composure. "Get into the bathroom," she hisses, "and lock the door. Now."

"But—"

"I will take care of them. Do it!" Lucie shoves me towards the bathroom door, then grabs my extra clothes and stuffs them underneath her sofa. My hands tremble as I lock the bathroom door and then lean against it, listening intently.

"It's six in the morning," Lucie says loudly, probably shouting through the door. "Do you need something?"

"Can I use your restroom?"

I'm pretty sure my heart is literally in my mouth right now...

"It's not available." Lucie's voice is surprisingly firm. "Ask someone else, please."

There is no more sound. Slowly I begin to breathe again, and then Lucie knocks on the door.

"Elvira?" she calls softly. "It's me. It's safe now."

I unlock the door and open it, and Lucie is there, smiling at me. I exhale in full relief.

"I was scared," I tell her honestly.

"So was I," she laughs. "Okay, if something like that happens again in the next ten minutes, there's a fire escape outside my bedroom window, okay? You can get out through there."

"What about you?" I ask pointedly.

Lucie shakes her head. "I should be okay as long as they don't find you."

"Are you su—"

I break off, staring at the hooded, masked woman who has just stepped out of Lucie's bedroom.

"Elvira, what's—" Lucie starts.

5

"Lucie, I don't want to hurt you. Please step aside."

The woman.

Why is her voice so familiar? And even her eyes?

How did she get in?

"No." Lucie turns slowly, still between me and the woman. "Who are you? Are you with the police?"

"Lucie, no!" I scream. I don't want her to get hurt! This is the same person who almost killed me at the hospital!

"Lucie, please." The woman raises her hand from her side. She's holding a gun. "I never wanted you to die."

"Then don't kill anybody." Lucie sounds confused. "What do you want?"

"I'm here for her." The woman gestures towards me, and my heart seems to stop beating.

"Never. Now put that gun down. The police will be here any minute."

The police?

She must mean Pietro.

"Lucie, I know exactly what you're trying to do. The police aren't coming. Just Pietro. Now, for the last time, get out of my way."

How does the woman know all this? Is this a nightmare?

Suddenly she runs forward, shoving Lucie aside and knocking me to the ground. I scream in pure terror. She has the end of the gun directly over my heart. I shut my eyes, sobbing. In a second I'll be—

There is another scream, but it isn't mine. Meanwhile Pietro is pounding on the door.

"Lucie, open up! What's happening!"

I open my eyes.

I'm covered in blood. But it isn't my blood. And it isn't the woman holding me down, it's Lucie.

Lucie?

"No…no…" The woman backs away, her eyes wide in horror. A few strands of graying red hair have escaped from her hood, and her mask has fallen off. Except for the scar running down her face, she looks like…

She looks like me.

"Lucie," I moan. I can't move and now I can't see because my eyes are full of tears. "Lucie… Please stop. Please stop! Lucie, are you… No, Lucie!"

"Stop!" the woman screams suddenly. It's like she, too, is in a nightmare. "*Stop!*"

She pulls out a knife, and her hand carries it down, into my face…no, it glances *off* my face, cutting it and then thudding into the floor.

"I hate you," the woman hisses in my face. "I *hate* you! I don't understand why…!"

There is a splitting sound as Pietro gets through the door. The woman looks up, runs across the room, and jumps out the window. There is a horrible noise of shattering glass.

I can't see Pietro, but I hear his heartrending cry.

"*Lucie, no!*"

6

Lucie Bernard was killed this morning in her apartment. The killer is unknown, but the police strongly suspect Pietro Dola, former FBI Agent and turncoat, or Elvira Thyme, a suspect in a top-secret case. Both are highly wanted and extremely dangerous criminals. Either should be reported on sight. Avoid contact. Here are two pictures of the suspects...

Pietro ran his hand through his hair and stared at the two pictures of himself and Elvira. So he was a suspect, was he? An extremely dangerous criminal?

Pietro was too broken to care.

Lucie had been killed... *Lucie*. She'd trusted him. She'd been willing to risk so much. She'd helped him—and paid for it with her life.

The guilt was Pietro's. In a way, the police were right. Pietro Dola *was* guilty for Lucie Bernard's life.

Lucie...

It wasn't supposed to end this way.

She had *trusted* him!

Pietro could've hated himself if it was allowed. But Elvira was still alive, even if she, too, was shocked and discouraged. He still had to protect her.

Pietro didn't know where he was going to get the willpower from. But it had to be there somewhere.

"You hungry, man?" His friend Stan stood in the doorway. Though he was autistic, a genius, and a bit of a daydreamer, Stan cared very deeply for the few people he chose to get to know. "I made tuna sandwiches for you and the girl."

Elvira was "the girl." Pietro couldn't help but smile slightly.

"I guess I should eat," he admitted. "Thanks, Stan."

The heavy-set man grinned like a toddler as he set the paper plate on Pietro's desk. "Food will make you feel better. Hope you like it. I'm not a professional cook."

"I'm grateful for everything," Pietro told him. "How's Elvira?"

"The girl? Oh, she's not talking much." *Probably because you don't talk,* Pietro thought to himself. Obliviously, Stan went on. "She liked the sandwiches, though."

Pietro took a bite and immediately marveled at Elvira's powers of deception. Pietro was going to have to make sure he did all the cooking from then on. He forced himself to take another bite.

"Did you figure out who did the job yet?" Stan asked. He was infamous for flipping light conversations into deep discussions with a single remark.

"What? No." Pietro sighed gloomily.

"Well, figure it out," Stan scowled. "You're good at that, FBI."

"I'm not FBI anymore, and this case has me stumped." Pietro bit his lip. "For once, Stan, I think it's impossible."

"Yeah, baloney," Stan laughed. "Nothing's impossible. You've told me that a million times." He thumped Pietro's back, ignoring the fact that the thin Italian-American nearly fell out of his chair.

"Keep figuring," he called after him as he left the room, closing the door behind him.

Pietro rubbed his back and stared morosely at the sandwich. He'd never wasted food and he wasn't going to now. He had some concern about the digestion of it this time, though. At least he knew Stan wouldn't try to kill him.

Deliberately, anyway.

6

04 June 2021
1408
Notes:
05 June 2021
0832
Disturbance at Present 19 October 2104
2018
Logged Off
Username:
Passcode:
Logged On
Travel: 05 June 2021 0833
[overlap]
Logged Off

Richard Lance was angry.

He'd never been made such a fool of before. He'd considered Pietro Dola to be one of the best men on the FBI force. Now Pietro Dola had defected and taken his research on the Slayer case with him, leaving the situation in a shambles. Not only that, but he'd taken the most highly prized leads with him.

Someone else had been killed: Lucie Bernard, who was supposed to have been Dola's fiancée. She'd been found brutally shot after one of her apartment neighbors had called the police about yelling and shattered glass. The apartment had been broken into, with both the door and the window destroyed. Lucie was on the floor, clinically dead. There was a bag of small women's clothes that were obviously not Lucie's.

Besides that everything seemed normal. As normal as it could be.

Lucie's funeral would probably have a large attendance, mostly due to public news, as she hadn't had any close family. The police would keep a close watch in case either Dola or Thyme tried to attend.

It was very confusing. Lucie Bernard had been on very good terms with both of the suspects. Or so it had seemed, anyway. There was no explanation for the murder, unless Lucie had tried to prevent Dola's escape with Thyme. The news jumped on the opportunity to make a martyr out of the young woman.

Meanwhile, the legal forces decided to announce that they actually didn't need Thyme anymore. They had all the information they needed. This was an attempt to neutralize any action taken by Dola—and to draw the Slayer out of hiding at the same time.

"You can't do something like this and get away with it, Agent Dola," Richard muttered to himself. "There will be a price to pay."

* * *

Lord, what is my confidence which I have in this life? or what is my greatest comfort amongst all things that appear under heaven?

I close the little pocket *Imitation* and shut my eyes.

Despite all the devastation, I find a strange peace of mind. Everything has come crashing down around me, but Faith still stands. I don't understand how, but I know it is true. God is still with me.

That doesn't mean I'm not buried under a crushing load of emotion, though. I feel guilt…so much guilt…though I know it's not my fault that Lucie and Pietro decided to help me. And yet…maybe if I had been stronger… Lucie and Pietro sacrificed their lives for me. Maybe Pietro is still alive, but Lucie is gone. Their happy married life together…never began. The little family has been shattered…before it became a family.

And it's all because of me.

Pietro hasn't said a word to me; I haven't even seen him since we arrived here last night. Only the big man who told me to call him Stan. He doesn't want to talk to me. He's told me nothing about Pietro.

I've been doing a lot of prayerful reading. A lot of writing in the notebook Pietro bought for me. Or maybe Lucie bought it. I found it in the purse they gave me. Along with my passport, a bar of chocolate, a fancy pen, a first aid kit, and a device that I don't recognize. I can't even figure out how to turn it on. If it even turns on. I gave up on it a long time ago.

But right now, I'm done reading and writing. I'm going to go find Pietro. I put the book down on the cot and stand up.

The door isn't locked, I discover with relief. I step out of the room and find myself in the long hallway through which I entered it last night. Hopefully Pietro's room is one of the two other doors. If not, I'll have to go upstairs, it looks like.

Stan said he was going to be busy all afternoon. Hopefully that means he's on a different floor?

I open the first door. Just as I remembered, it's the helicopter's hangar. No one is around, and the massive door is shut. I come back into the hallway and try the next door. It's locked.

Sighing, I head down the hallway towards the stairs. Five seconds later I am scared out of my skin by Pietro's question.

"Did you need something?"

He's right behind me! I scream, flipping out and punching him before I have time to think. Pietro gasps for breath.

"What was that for?" He's angry, I can tell. "What is wrong with you?"

"I'm sorry!" I back away and start crying. "I didn't mean to do that! You scared me!"

Thankfully, he seems to be over it. "I guess I should apologize, then. At least I don't have to worry about your reflexes. Are you looking for something, Elvira?"

"I was looking for you," I admit.

"Okay. Then come with me, before Stan freaks out."

I follow Pietro back to the door that had been locked. It's designed like a nice little office, and it actually seems very much like Pietro's style. I bet he's worked here before.

He closes the door behind us and gestures for me to sit on the bed. "Alright. Why were you looking for me, Elvira?"

Suddenly I start crying again. After all this…he wonders why I look for him?

Pietro's eyes open wide, just like the time I hugged him when he came to visit me. "Good heavens," he mutters. "Elvira—please—"

"I'm sorry," I cry, rubbing my sleeve across my eyes. "I just wanted to tell you…I'm sorry!"

"Elvira, it's *not* your fault!" Pietro is aghast. "I thought you knew that!"

"I'm still sorry for you! I wish I could go back in time—and—"

"Elvira, please listen to me." Pietro looks at me seriously. "It's not your fault. I don't hate you. I'm not mad at you. Yes, I miss Lucie, and I'm angry at myself for getting her into this. But none of that is your fault, okay? And we're going to live through this."

He bites his lip. "Impossible as it seems, we are going to go on. I think you and I are going to leave the country. For now, anyway. Until things have calmed down, the Slayer is caught, and the legal forces are ready to listen to reason."

"Pietro, you've ruined your career for me, haven't you?" I ask him.

"My career is worth nothing if I can't protect you." Pietro's voice is firm. "What is the purpose of law enforcement if law enforcement doesn't protect the people it was created to help thrive? Elvira, our government is corrupted, and so long as it's that way, I won't be a part of it. This is a personal decision of mine, and you are not to blame. Do you understand that?"

I nod slowly.

"Now, Elvira, I'm not forcing you to do anything. I've assumed you want to be redeemed as opposed to being used as bait for the Slayer. But if you don't want to do it my way, or you don't want to do it at all, you have only to tell me. I will help you as long as it falls within my moral code. A moral code we share."

"No, I trust you," I tell him.

Pietro winces. "Right. Then we're going to work together."

I blink in surprise. "You mean *I* can actually help you?" I honestly feel more like dead weight.

"Yes. Elvira, I didn't…I didn't want to talk about this last night, but I need you to give me every last detail you noticed about the killer. The Slayer, I'm assuming. I need every single piece of information. Whether it seems relevant or not."

Now, *this*, I was expecting at some point.

"They came in through the fire escape outside Lucie's bedroom window, I think," I begin.

"How do you know there's a fire escape there?" Pietro questions.

"Lucie told me, right before, in case something happened."

"Okay, and what was the first thing the killer did?"

"She came out—"

"*She?*" Pietro gets excited.

"I saw her face," I admit.

His eyes are so intent they almost scare me. "Describe it to me."

"She had a scar…right here, actually." I trace the bandage on my cheek where the knife barely missed me last night. "Her eyes are hazel-blue…like mine, I guess. Her hair is a bit darker—"

"It's red?" Pietro seems confused.

I nod. "With a bit of white near the scalp. She was wearing a dark hoodie, dark skirt, black combat boots… She had at least a knife and a gun, but she could've had more. Oh…and her hands were gloved, but something shone through the glove on her left hand." I can remember that vividly from when the knife came down. "Something…blue. Blue light. Right about where…" I glance down at my left wrist. "Where I wear my watch."

That's odd. Most people don't wear their watch the way I do.

"So, in other words, she looked a lot like you." Pietro bites his lip.

"Yes…" The thought takes me by surprise. "I guess so. But she was much older than me."

"How old, would you say?"

"Maybe sixty? I'm not good with ages."

"Okay. Now, keep telling me what happened. Start when the Slayer stepped out of Lucie's bedroom."

* * *

"Here are the coordinates, Stan. Thanks for everything."

"Come back safe and soon, Pietro." Stan grinned. "Now, get back there and buckle up. The weather doesn't look good." Pietro nodded wordlessly and stepped out of the helicopter cockpit. He took one of the three seats in the back, just behind Elvira.

"Are you ready?" Pietro asked her, seeing that she was buckled and had her purse.

"Yes." Elvira smiled back at him. "Are you?"

Pietro nodded again, buckling himself in. He leaned back and closed his eyes as the engines began to roar. He had a lot to think about during the two hours they'd be flying—to the Canada border.

Pietro had permitted himself the luxury of not thinking about the case until now. Now he'd have a good two hours to solve it and figure out what to do. It couldn't be *that* complicated.

After half an hour or so, though, Pietro decided it was. So these were the facts—as he saw them—and they didn't make sense together.

The Slayer was a woman, in looks and habits much like Elvira herself. However, she could not reasonably be any close relation to Elvira.

She was a cold, emotionless killer—except when it came to her current target. When face to face with Elvira, she became emotional and confused.

The Slayer had an uncannily accurate knowledge of exactly *what* was happening *when.* She also had an apparently personal knowledge of Lucie, and possibly Pietro. The very thought gave Pietro the chills—he, too, *had* to know the person.

The Slayer had escaped an exploding vehicle, leaving no trace. She hated Elvira...and, apparently, neither of the two understood why.

Those were the facts—now for the implications.

When it came to Elvira, the Slayer was not her normal self. She had not actually intended to kill Lucie. That had been unintentional.

All three—Pietro, Lucie, and Elvira, either knew the Slayer very well, or she had been studying them very, very closely. Pietro shook his head. He didn't know any redhead women...besides Elvira, anyway.

The older woman was either able to sense the future, or had some amazing deduction skills. And lastly...she was not going to give up until either she'd been caught or Elvira was dead.

The last two thoughts especially worried Pietro. If the Slayer knew they were going to Canada...they wouldn't be safe, even there.

He hoped desperately that he was wrong and that the enemy had just been lucky so far.

"Pietro?" Elvira was talking to him.

Pietro jumped, startled. "What is it?"

"Where are we going?"

Pietro pursed his lips. "Canada border."

"Are they going to let us through? Or are we going to cross illegally?" Elvira looked distinctly uncomfortable with the second option.

The Italian-American laughed. "We're going to cross the normal way." Suddenly a thought struck him. The Slayer had used the fire exit only after Lucie had told Elvira about it...

Pietro smiled faintly. "Don't worry. Our papers aren't on the American records, so to catch us, they'd have to report us to the US government. And we'll not give them any reason to do that, right?"

Elvira grinned back. "Right."

7

Pietro was highly relieved that the border crossing had gone so smoothly. He'd half expected Elvira's picture to be questioned, at the very least. But they were waved through without any trouble.

And now, on a train to Quebec, they were safe. From the American legal forces, anyway. Pietro finally felt that he could breathe. He knew the FBI net very well—and they'd escaped it!

Besides which, his little test on Elvira had gone as he'd expected it to. If the Canadian police had stopped them for no apparent reason, Pietro would've been almost totally certain that somehow the Slayer was getting information from Elvira. Now he was reassured...though a small shred of doubt still remained.

If it wasn't the Slayer's intention to keep them in America, she would've had no reason to warn the Canadian police. She could kill them just as easily in Canada as in the United States. Pietro scowled to himself.

"What's wrong?" Elvira asked, but just then, the former FBI agent's attention was taken up by a woman who was trying to get onto the train.

"Wait, please!" she called in American English, seemingly materializing from the crowd on the station platform. She was in a yellow shirt, with a black sweatshirt tied around her waist. Her hair was tucked up into her had, but Pietro could've sworn it was dark red. He glanced at Elvira, and she joined him at the train window.

The woman got onto the train, and Pietro bit his lip. "Elvira...I think we need to relocate ourselves."

He looked at the teenager and saw that her face was an almost bloodless white.

"It's her," Elvira breathed. "There is no scar...but it *is* her."

"Makeup," Pietro nodded, picking up his heavy carpetbag. "Okay, we're going to get off at the next station. Thankfully, it should only be a couple of minutes."

"Pietro..." Elvira looked up at him, her hazel-blue eyes filled with fear—but for Pietro, not for herself. "Please, go on without me."

"Absolutely not." Pietro chose not to get emotional at times like these. He'd been in tight spots before and he didn't intend to start running from them now. Especially when he was pretty sure he wouldn't be intentionally targeted. "We stick together, El—Cassandra. Cassie. We stick together."

"Pietro, she's coming." Elvira's eyes filled with tears. "I know she is. *You* know she is."

Pietro took her hand. "Come on," he said firmly. "Let's get moving."

They got a few train sections away before the next stop was reached and the two got out before anyone else. Pietro pulled Elvira into a coffee shop and told her to go use the restroom. Casually, he ordered a dark espresso for himself and sat down to drink it slowly. He'd notify Elvira when he thought it was safe to leave—via the rather simple device he'd given her and explained to her on the helicopter. It was incapable of being hacked and could only be used to contact Pietro himself.

Pietro caught his breath as the woman came into the café. It seemed that she glanced his way before ordering the exact same drink he had.

He exhaled slowly in something between surprise and fear as the woman took the seat opposite him. It was a two-person table and her action was obviously deliberate and calculated.

"Hello, Pietro," the woman breathed.

If he was honest with himself, Pietro hadn't expected anything else. "Are you going to kill me now?"

He couldn't help but notice the strange blue-glowing watch on the woman's left wrist. This had to be the Slayer, and Pietro didn't know whether he was more terrified or fulfilled.

The woman shook her head. "You don't understand. I never wanted you to die, Pietro."

Suddenly her eyes filled with tears. "I missed you...Pietro...I missed you so much..."

Pietro slowly backed away in his chair. This was...this was totally unexpected and uncharacteristic of the Slayer. Her face was so familiar. It was literally the same as Elvira's. Pietro kept thinking he was talking to Elvira, every instant. He shook the thought off. No, this was the Slayer, and she was trying to manipulate him.

"Pietro, please pull the device out of your bag and tell me it's okay to come out now."

Pietro stared. *What* exactly was the Slayer trying to say? Tell her? Tell Elvira? Tell Elvira, the Slayer, that it was okay to come out now? So that she, the Slayer, could kill herself, Elvira?

Suddenly it all clicked for Pietro.

"No," he said simply, and Elvira frowned.

"I don't want to have to take it from you. Just do it, Pietro. Please."

Her hazel-blue eyes were begging, pleading.

Pietro hesitated, then looked away firmly. "No."

"I didn't wa—"

He locked eyes with her. "You don't have to. Give it up, Elvira."

"So you've guessed it." Elvira stood up. "Pietro, maybe you don't fully understand yet. You never fully told me. But I'm going to end the Slayer...before she becomes the monster I am. Think about that, Pietro."

She turned and walked out of the café, leaving her full cup of coffee on the small table. Pietro watched her go, then continued staring out the window absently.

So now he know the truth. But it was a harder truth that he'd ever had to accept before.

The vulnerable girl he'd given himself to protect? The young woman Lucie had died for?

They did so much to save her...and she was growing up to become a serial killer. To become the Slayer. To end by coming back in time to kill herself.

What could Pietro do? He couldn't help Elvira commit suicide...even in circumstances like these. He couldn't *let* her, either.

He could only continue to try to protect her...regardless of what the future seemed to hold. He could only hope and pray for the best.

Pietro took another sip of coffee, then pulled the device out of his bag to let Elvira know it was safe to come back. A couple of minutes later she found his table and sat down. "Whose coffee is this?" she frowned.

"Yours," Pietro shrugged.

"Did she leave?" Elvira looked around the restaurant.

"Yes. Sit down, please." Pietro wasn't in a mood for much talking.

He watched Elvira as she took a sip of the coffee and made a face.

"You'll get used to it," Pietro commented thoughtfully.

"Pietro, what's wrong?" Elvira looked confused.

"Elvira..."

He couldn't tell her she was going to be a serial killer, could he? That she *was* the Slayer?

That might only cement her future.

Pietro yawned. "I'm tired. Are you ready to go?"

"Yes. Did you pay for this or can I—"

"Throw it away, I don't care." Pietro finished his own espresso and stood up. All semblance of fatigue disappeared from his olive-toned face. "Let's go catch the next train to Quebec."

The two walked outside together. The next second, they weren't together. Pietro didn't really see what happened. He just knew that one instant Elvira was beside him and the next instant she wasn't.

"Dai!" he hissed as someone else on the sidewalk screamed. Elvira had been shoved off the raised platform, onto the train tracks.

Pietro moved faster than he'd ever thought possible. The train was coming...he heard its warning whistle as he leaned dangerously far off the platform.

"Elvira!"

She was up on her feet now, grabbing at the four-feet-high platform. Pietro grabbed her hands and began to pull her up. Some man behind him added his support, and soon Elvira was back on the platform.

The man who'd helped Pietro was now yelling in French for everyone to stand back. Elvira stayed close to Pietro and brushed herself off. Pietro was pretty sure he saw her wince, but now was not the time to worry about small injuries. He had a much bigger concern: the Canadian police.

"We're going to file a report," Pietro whispered to Elvira. "Act like you have no idea."

"We can't lie." Elvira scowled.

Pietro bit his lip. "Okay, then we won't file a report. Tell them you lost your balance."

"But—"

"You did." Pietro half-smiled. "You lost your balance because the Slayer pushed you."

Elvira laughed weakly. "Got it."

* * *

I'm awake in the hotel room bed...I can't sleep. Maybe it's the coffee from earlier, maybe not. Maybe it's just the fact that I'm scared.

The Slayer is hunting me...and I feel strongly that they'll be trying again, and soon. It seems that nothing Pietro or I can do will stop her... I feel strangely alone. Pietro has been acting strangely since we took the train. He won't talk much...I hope it's not my fault...I can't think of why...maybe because I tossed the coffee?

No. That's stupid. Pietro's not like that.

I can't see him right now, but I know he's sitting by the door, watching. He doesn't think it's safe for me to have my own room, so he's not going to sleep. He's just sitting there by the door… I wish he didn't have to stay up. Maybe he'll sleep tomorrow. He hasn't told me any of his plans…

* * *

I wake up with a start. I don't know the time, but I hear voices and the light is on. I slip out of bed—then freeze. Pietro is talking to…the Slayer.

"Don't you see that your machine won't let you?" Pietro is asking. "It's pointless to keep trying. You should try to *change* the future, instead of simply deleting it."

"How? If I change the future…I can't go back and fix it."

"And if you kill yourself, you can't come back to kill yourself. Be reasonable, Elvira."

Elvira? Come back to kill myself?

What is going on…?

"Will you help me, then?"

"I will."

None of this makes sense. Pietro is going to help…the Slayer? Do what?

"Shh." This time the voice is much closer to me. A hand reaches up onto the bed, stifling my scream.

I hear a quiet laugh. "If you want to stay alive, little girl, don't move."

* * *

"Will you help me, then?"

Pietro held out his hand to take the older woman's. "I will."

Gray-haired Elvira hesitated. "Pietro…"

"What?"

She took a deep breath. "I remember…that this is when you died."

Pietro felt a chill run down his spine. "I…died?"

Suddenly her eyes opened wide as she understood. "Pietro...*please*... please don't hate me. Tell me... Tell me that only *I* can destroy myself."

But then she frowned. "No...you didn't have time to say anything."

Pietro smiled rather unexpectedly. "I didn't?"

He dropped to the ground as a bullet sped through his hair into the wall where his forehead had just been. Pietro felt the sting, but at least he wasn't dead. Not yet, anyway. And hopefully not at all.

He reached for his gun, then scowled darkly as he remembered he hadn't been able to take it through the Canadian customs. There was only his pepper spray and a small knife he'd bought that afternoon.

Someone jumped on top of him, and Pietro cried out in pain as they shot him in the back, once, twice, thrice. Somehow he managed one of his professional twists and found himself grappling with a very strong, scarred red-haired woman.

Yet another Elvira, apparently. Pietro felt dizzy.

She pinned him down. Pietro managed to pull out his knife, but the Slayer didn't give him a chance to use it. It caught his hand as she threw it away, and cut his arm terribly. Pietro was gasping in agony.

Somewhere behind the Slayer he saw...Elvira. She had betrayed him.

She grew up to kill him. She was watching him die, now. Doing nothing to help him.

Pietro's face twisted in pain and mental anguish.

"Elvira!" he screamed. The Slayer paused a moment, the first twinge of emotion coming into her cold face. Behind her, Elvira's face was white as she caught her breath.

"Elvira, this is—*for you!*" Pietro gasped out in a last effort. His vision was going now.

"Liar!" the Slayer screamed, pressing her gun to his forehead.

Pietro made an instantaneous Act of Contrition. This was it and he knew it.

* * *

I throw myself between the Slayer and Pietro, knocking the gun away from his head before the new Slayer can shoot.

"No!" I can hear myself screaming. "I don't want to! I don't *want* to!"

I knock all the breath out of Pietro, but he opens his eyes again.

"Elvira…you don't have to."

His eyes meet mine.

"You don't have to."

A hole appears in his chest, over his heart. Pietro half-sighs…and then nothing. The light goes out of his eyes.

"Pietro!" I scream.

The Slayer pulls me away, shoving me hard against the wall. My head hits it with a sickening thud.

"Give it up," the Slayer hisses. "It's over. It's *over*. Nothing will change. Now you are safe."

"She *will* be safe…when you are gone."

The Slayer spins around, and I follow her gaze to the other Slayer. The first Slayer. The one Pietro was talking to. The…the third Elvira.

The real Slayer, the cold-blooded killer, laughs coldly as she stands in front of me. "I am the future. You're just a shadow of what could've been. You can't kill me and you can't kill her. Get lost, El."

"If I were only a shadow, I wouldn't be here to fight you for the future, Vira."

Suddenly "El" pounces, but "Vira" whips out a knife and blocks her halfway. She grabs El's wrist and drives the knife deep into the blue-glowing watch they're both wearing.

El gasps in pain as the glow fades, but Vira laughs. "Now you're stuck and helpless."

"You're not going to kill yourself," El says dryly, but Vira's face twists into a sneer.

"Sixty years is long enough for someone like me." She lifts her hand with her gun, and shoots twice.

I watch my older self fall, but suddenly Vira grabs me by the shoulders.

"This is how you die!" she screams. "This is how *I* die! We are your future!"

The room fills with blue light, coming from Vira's watch, and I pass out.

* * *

"Time for some history," Vira says sweetly.

I'm sitting on the sofa in her living room, a starkly bare place in her starkly bare house in Kazakhstan. I woke up here five minutes ago. Vira got glasses of water for both of us, informing me at the same time that I am now in her "present"—nineteen years after my own. I have a splitting headache and my emotions are totally numb. But at least I'm starting to be less confused.

I piece together what I know. Lucie is dead. Pietro is dead. I am nineteen years in the future.

"You—I—found Vremya five years ago." Vira points towards the watch on her wrist. "Vremya is our handy time traveling machine. She's one out of three existing. They're made from crystals from the exploding core of Neptune."

I shake my head dizzily, but she keeps going anyway.

"Technically I should still be in prison for killing Pietro and Lucie. I just traveled to the future and broke myself out. Thankfully I traveled far enough ahead in time to see what the world becomes. It's heading in a bad direction, dear."

She pats my back, and I flinch. "Ergo, I'm now using Vremya to go back and undo the damage. Ergo the criminal whom the FBI call the Slayer. You don't become a bad guy, Elvira. I'm not a bad guy. I'm trying to save the world."

I simply stare at her.

Vira sighs. "Let me show you."

8

ira is looking down at me. Her face is covered in disgust. "Why do you keep passing out?"

"I'm not…the one…wearing the time machine," I mumble weakly.

She kicks me. "Get up. It's not safe to hang around here."

Vira holds out her hand, and I take it and pull myself up slowly. I look around, ignoring the hammering in my head. We're standing in a rainy, dark, back alley. The perfect dystopian picture.

"This was going to have been a lot worse." Vira grimaces. "Then I shot one of their top masterminds. The future is better every time I travel to it. Come on, let's get out of here before someone finds us."

I follow her down the alley and into some low-roofed tavern. The room spins around me as she leads me to a table and gestures for me to sit down. "I'm going to get something," she tells me. "Do you—no, I didn't. Got it."

She walks away, leaving me leaning against the back of the chair. I have to get away from her, somehow…

I can't do anything, I realize. I'm stuck here…in the future. The thought hits me like a thunderbolt.

Now there is really nothing I can do to change anything. It's too late.

But wait, there *is* one thing I can do, I decide. Keep Vira busy.

She can't kill me because I am her past. But she can't let me get away from her, either. That means I can do what I like and get away with it.

I open my eyes. Vira is ordering some kind of drink at the bar counter. There are a lot of people here, so I am pretty sure I can sneak out unnoticed.

I get only halfway to the door when someone grabs my arm. My reflexes kick into action and I swing around, punching whoever it is before I can think. The man grunts but doesn't let go. Instead, his grip tightens. I stare in horror. He's six feet tall and covered in tattoos. And the expression on his face isn't a friendly one.

"So, shrimp." His lips curl into an expression of disgust. "What was that for? I jes wanted another drink."

He thinks I'm a waitress? Anyway, I'm in trouble now. Some of the people around us have stopped talking to watch. Someone laughs coarsely, drunkenly. I bite my lip.

If these people kill me, then Vira ceases to exist. Which means she has to protect me.

I gasp for breath as the man lands his other hand in my stomach. "Answer me, peanut!"

"Sorry, I got scared," I manage to say, but it isn't enough.

"I'll scare you, you…you rat!"

Someone grabs his free arm. It's some young man. He's dressed in dirty, worn, dark combat-type clothes, but his face is kind. "Leave her alone," he says. But the awakened wasp's nest isn't finished with me.

"Stay outta this, Dola!" My heart skips a beat. Dola?

It's not Pietro. But the face is similar. How… Did Pietro have family?

Meanwhile, my savior gives the drunken man a quick, hard uppercut under the chin. "That's just a taste," he barks roughly as the man cries out and lets go of me. "See me outside later if you want more."

My arm and my chest hurt, but I smile at my rescuer. "Thanks…"

"It's Damion. Damion Dola," he grins back, and I catch my breath. His eyes…are Lucie's eyes. "Are you…are you okay?"

"My name is Elvira," I breathe.

And then Vira pulls me away. She's furious.

"Get away from her, you street thief!" she hisses. "Get lost…Dola? What was your name?" She glares at him.

And then Damion is gone. Vira looks like she'd like to chase after him, but she glances back at me and changes her mind.

"I'd love to kill you slowly, right here."

"But you can't," I point out. My brain cells are starting to function again, and I'm getting a bit more spunky.

"No, but Lukkie can do it for me." She gestures towards the guy I tangled with, then grabs my arm and pulls me towards the door, her drink in hand. "Try that again and I just might."

I don't try to come up with a response as she leads me through the dark and dreary streets. I look up and realize that it's not twilight—the sky is clouded with fumes.

"What time is it?" I ask after a few minutes, when Vira seems to have calmed down a bit.

"19 October 2104—8:18 PM."

So it *is* night after all?

"We're going to go visit someone." Vira laughs. "Someone…who knows us both very well. Hmm," she murmurs, "so Pietro and Lucie got married and had a child before they died? I wonder what did that."

"What?" I stare at her. "Oh. You're right. They did."

"And his name is Damion Dola."

I try to remember. Yes, she's right. Lucie and Pietro were married before I met them. I never knew about their child, though. But the thought is somewhat comforting to me, that there is something of them left in the world. The thought strikes me that Damion looked rather young. Then I realize what is happening, and drive the thought away quickly.

Vira can't read my mind, but she *can* remember what happens in my life. I try hard to think about how broken up I feel, and succeed pretty well. So well, in fact, that after we've been walking for twenty minutes, my steps begin to drag…and the world starts spinning.

* * *

I wake up and at first have no idea where I am. Then I remember. It's the sofa back in Vira's living room. The lights are off. I guess Vira must be sleeping, too. Where, I don't know.

I sit up slowly, remembering everything. Pietro and Lucie. The Slayer. The past...and the future. The future that I have to stop somehow. The future that is the present.

The present...but I am still myself, aren't I? I might be in the future, but my timeline is still the present. The present that can change.

If only I know how...

I slip off the sofa and head for the front door. It's locked, and probably has an alarm rigged, so I sneak out the kitchen window. I find myself on a deserted town street lit only by street lights. Where, I don't know. When? The oven clock read something after 3:00 in the morning.

No wonder no one is around.

I walk down the street. I don't know where I'm going, I just know I want to get away from Vira, while I can. If she wakes up or takes the time to remember, she'll know where to find me. But I just want to be alone for now. Some time later, I see a public neighborhood park. I head into it, jumping as the metal gate clangs shut behind me.

Sitting down on a bench, I pull my hot pink hoodie jacket tightly about me. It brings back memories...this is the jacket Pietro bought for me. It feels like ages ago since I put it on and Lucie smiled to see me in it, but it's really been only a few days. I pull up the hoodie as a tear slips down my cheek and onto the bandage.

It seems that I sit there for hours, thinking and wondering. Wondering... how to change the present-past. How...without Pietro, Lucie, Stan...

I think of Damion, and smile, a bittersweet smile. There's no way I'll find him now.

Someone slips onto the bench beside me, and I sigh.

"It hurts, doesn't it," Vira murmurs. "That's why I chose to forget. You might as well start forgetting now."

"I will never forget," I reply softly. "These memories will keep me from becoming like you."

Vira laughs. "It's not a question of *becoming* like me, little girl. It's a question of getting older. That's all."

I feel sick. She can't be right…she simply can't. If I reject this future…I don't have to live it.

Pietro's last words echo in my mind. *Elvira, you don't have to.* And suddenly I know.

"No," I say aloud. "I don't care what the future holds. I don't care what the government does to me. I'm going to save my soul and help people. That's what I'm going to do, for the rest of my life."

Vira looks confused. "This *is* the rest of yo—"

I stand up and throw my head back, looking up at the stars. "This isn't the present. This is just a nightmare. And it's time for me to wake up."

1

What happened? I don't know… I'm still half asleep, I guess… My arm hurts, my neck and back, too… And there's a bandage on my face.

Where am I? This is totally not my bedroom ceiling. Tile, with lights that hurt my eyes…

"Where am I?" I manage to whisper. My lips are covered in something dried…blood? My face hurts to move.

I blink as someone moves into view. A nurse?

Am I in the hospital?

"You're awake!" she smiles brightly. "How are you feeling, Ms. Thyme? Do you remember what happened?"

Suddenly I sit bolt upright as the memories come back to me. "Where are my parents?" I ask urgently, panic in my voice. "Where are they?"

"Hey, you're going to be okay, Ms. Thyme. Lie back down, please. You'll get to see your parents later."

But the smile has already faded from her face.

"No," I scream. "No!"

I shut my eyes tightly, reliving the crash. Mom and Dad are in the front of the car… I'm in the back, laughing about how Dad knew exactly what coffee I wanted. It tastes so good… My Dad is awesome.

Then we turn the corner. Impact.

Mom and Dad smash forward but their seat belts stop them. I slam my head on the back of Dad's seat and black out, my own scream fading away in my ears. The nurse is tapping my shoulder. I open my eyes again and let the tears flow.

"I'm sorry, Elvira."

Her voice is so coldly gentle. I hate it. Or do I just hate the words?

"Your parents didn't make it."

* * *

I don't know what to do.

I'm lying awake, even though it's past 2 AMam. I'm not crying anymore. My eyes feel dead. My mind feels even more dead.

Please tell me this is just a dream… My parents are dead. I have no other relatives. I'm only eighteen. I haven't even started my first job.

I am all alone.

My parents… I squeeze my eyes shut, grabbing my chest. My heart hurts… O God, help me… What am I going to do?

Pray. That's what I'm going to do. Because my life isn't over yet. And I'm not broken.

It's just beginning.

* * *

Two weeks later is my third day of work. I'm helping out at a children's daycare. Everything's gone unbelievably well in the past two weeks, considering the turn my life has taken.

I was well enough to attend my parents' funeral Mass. Everyone has been extremely supportive in helping me get on my own two feet. I'm sharing an apartment with a friend from the church. Father Cyprian has helped me immensely, and I'm beginning to get over the depression. My job is definitely going to help with that. It's very invigorating to work with children.

Today, though, one of the children runs up to me when it's time for their parents to pick them up. I smile at cute little Damian Dola. He's only four.

"Ms. Thyme!" he pleads. "Can you come meet my daddy?"

I look around. "Umm, I guess so."

Damion grabs my hand and pulls me outside, to one of the cars. I raise my eyebrows slightly as I see that it's equipped with alert lights, though they're off. Damion's dad must be a cop of some sorts.

The driver opens his door and steps out. He looks Italian-American, and several years older than me.

"Daddy, this is Ms. Thyme!" Damion tells him, and the man smiles, holding out his hand to shake mine.

"Nice to meet you. I'm Pietro Dola. My son has talked a lot about you in the past few days."

I shake his hand back, noting how strong it is. "My name's Elvira Thyme. Damion's a very good little boy and I'm happy to help take care of him."

Some of the happy sparkle vanishes from Pietro's eyes. "Thank you for helping him. He lost his mother two weeks ago."

I feel the numb pain in my chest flare up, and my eyes fill with tears that I quickly blink back. "I'm sorry…"

Suddenly I say something I never thought I'd tell a random stranger. "Me, too."

Pietro's eyes fill with compassion as Damion wraps himself around his dad's legs. "Ms. Thyme…I'm sorry. I really am."

I force a smile. "Thank you. I appreciate it."

"Do you want my number? If you ever need help, let me know."

He fumbles in his pocket and pulls out a business card, handing it to me. *Pietro Dola. FBI.*

It seems strangely familiar. There's a funny sense that I've met Pietro before. But…for the life of me, I can't remember when.

I look at him, and he nods.

"Please contact me if you need anything. My wife would've been happy to help you."

"Thank you. I'd better head back in, now. God bless you." I smile and bend down to wave at Damion.

"God bless you, too," Pietro tells me. "Goodbye."

Not many people say that nowadays, do they. I walk away, reflecting that I've just found yet another treasure of a friend.

Someone walks up the sidewalk towards me. "Do you happen to know an Elvira Thyme? A young woman working here?"

I stare in confusion. I have no idea who this woman is, but she's dressed like any normal policewoman.

"Yes…I am Elvira Thyme." I hesitate. "Is something wrong?"

"Can you come with me, please?"

She leads me to her car. "There's been a package found addressed to you but mailed a few years back. Can I see your ID, please?"

I hand her my license, and she compares the address. "Looks like it's yours," the woman decides. "Here you go."

I look over the package. It's old and battered, with no return address. "I never ordered this…"

"Maybe it was a gift." The woman smiles. "Have a good day, Miss Thyme."

"You, too."

I walk back into the daycare building and go to get my purse from my locker. One of my coworkers waves at me. "Bye, Elvira."

"Bye." I grab my purse and the package and head outside again, to my car this time.

By the time I get to the apartment, I've forgotten all about the package. Then, as I get out, something inside of it starts beeping. I freeze, then back away quickly. If it's a bomb…

The beeping stops, and nothing happens.

You're just paranoid, I tell myself, and reach into the car to pull out the package.

I walk into my apartment and put my purse on the kitchen table. My friend isn't back yet and she won't be for a while… I find a knife and open the package.

It's just a watch…an old-fashioned style watch band with a watch face that is definitely not old fashioned. It lights up as I look at it…a light blue glow tells me that the time is 6:02 PM.

I pick it up and fasten it on my left wrist, just above my normal, plain old watch. It fits perfectly.

I catch my breath as a million memories fly through my mind. Blood…fear…anger…

Pietro. Lucie.

"Elvira?"

My companion is standing in the doorway.

"Are you okay?"

I slide the watch off and take a deep breath. What *was* all that?

"Yeah, I'm okay."

The End

About the Author

⁕

Gabrielle Marie Kozak is an American author whose fiction explores pressure, endurance, and the cost of refusing to surrender oneself to oppressive systems. Her debut, *The Trooper Series*, began as a body of work written before she graduated high school and introduced her recurring focus on individual sovereignty under strain.

The eldest of nine children, Gabrielle spent nearly two years as a religious sister before turning her attention fully to writing and publishing. Her stories center on those who carry responsibility, those who break beneath it, and those who survive when systems fail.

She lives in Nebraska and loves writing, coffee, and all things Poland.

Website: **gmariaek.com**

Also by Gabrielle Marie Kozak

Thank you for reading!

If this story stayed with you, I would be grateful if you'd consider leaving a short review. Reviews help books like this find the readers who need them.

Your time, your attention, and your support truly matter.

If you'd like to continue reading my work, **The Trooper Series** is the best place to start.

Trooper A1: The Purple Blitzkrieg is the first book in the series.

Trooper A1: The Purple Blitzkrieg
SHE LOST HER BROTHER - JUST NOT THE WAY SHE THOUGHT.

Moira Whyte refuses to believe the **bloody evidence** that confirms her brother's death. Instead, she begins to hack into **Encephalon**, the underground network built to **subjugate the entire world.**

She's right. Her brother isn't dead.

He's worse than dead.

Trooper A2: "Little Trooper"
HE WAS RAISED TO BE SAFE. HE WAS BORN TO BE SOMETHING ELSE.

When **Evolet Whyte** first meets his real parents and siblings, they **shatter** his view on life–forever. **His mother has a story.** Does he trust her–or does he believe what **history itself** tells him?

The **truth won't wait** for him to find it in the skyscrapers and the classrooms. It's coming to find him–and it could **destroy** both Evolet and his new-found family.

To survive, Evolet must **discover and awaken** the "Little" Trooper within.